Ninette of Sin Street

Ninette of Sin Street

a novella by Vitalis Danon

EDITED WITH AN INTRODUCTION AND NOTES BY
LIA BROZGAL AND SARAH ABREVAYA STEIN

TRANSLATED BY
JANE KUNTZ

STANFORD UNIVERSITY PRESS • STANFORD, CALIFORNIA

Stanford University Press
Stanford, California

Ninette of Sin Street was first published in 1938 in French under the title *Ninette de la rue du Péché: une nouvelle populiste* by Editions de la Kahéna, Tunis, Tunisia. "A Visit to the Jews of Djerba (Travel Notes)" was first published in 1929 in French under the title "Chez les Juifs de Djerba (Notes de voyage)" in the volume *La hara conte: Folklore judéo-tunisien,* by J. Véhel, Ryvel, and V. Danon, Les Editions Ivrit, Paris, France. The original French versions of "A Flaneur in Sfax, 1918," "Mission to Gabès, 1937," and "A Swan Song, 1963" are preserved in the archives of the Alliance Israélite Universelle (Paris).

Printed in the United States of America on acid-free, archival-quality paper

Library of Congress Cataloging-in-Publication Data

Names: Danon, Vitalis, 1897–1969, author. | Brozgal, Lia Nicole, 1972–
  editor, writer of introduction. | Stein, Sarah Abrevaya, editor, writer of introduction. |
Kuntz, Jane, translator.
Title: Ninette of Sin Street : a novella / by Vitalis Danon ; edited with an introduction
  and notes by Lia Brozgal and Sarah Abrevaya Stein; translated by Jane Kuntz.
Other titles: Ninette de la rue du Péché. English
Description: Stanford, California : Stanford University Press, 2017. | "First published
  in 1938 in French under the title Ninette de la rue du Péché: une nouvelle populiste by
  Éditions de la Kahéna, Tunis, Tunisia." |
Includes bibliographical references and index.
Identifiers: LCCN 2016043167 (print) | LCCN 2016044145 (ebook) |
ISBN 9781503601567 (cloth : alk. paper) | ISBN 9781503602137 (pbk. : alk. paper) |
ISBN 9781503602298 (ebook) Subjects: LCSH: Jews—Tunisia—Fiction. | Tunisia—
Fiction. | LCGFT: Novellas.
Classification: LCC PQ3989.D3 N513 2017 (print) | LCC PQ3989.D3 (ebook) |
DDC 843/.912—dc23
LC record available at https://lccn.loc.gov/2016043167

Typeset by Bruce Lundquist in 11/15 Adobe Garamond Pro

CONTENTS

Ninette of
Sin Street

COLONIAL TUNISIA FROM THE GUTTER UP

Ninette of Sin Street peers up at colonial society from the gutter, rather than down from the balcony of high politics. Sin Street is a place where sex and sexual violence, parenting and patronage, and desperation and desire constantly intermingle; Ninette, however, is invested in the importance of a safe place to sleep, an education for her illegitimate child, and the challenge of erasing the taint of a sullied past. In short, *Ninette of Sin Street* is about ordinary, everyday life and, as such, is a study in power relations as they took shape on the ground and in the street, amidst the intricacies of colonial rule, religious difference, and class discrepancy.

Published in Tunis in 1938, *Ninette of Sin Street* is one of the first works of Tunisian fiction in French, and one of a small corpus of stories written by Jews about the local, mostly poor, Jews of Tunisia.[1] Having come to Tunisia as a teacher under the aegis of the Franco-Jewish organization the Alliance Israélite Universelle (AIU), *Ninette*'s author, Vitalis Danon, was an Ottoman Jew who quickly adopted, and was to a large degree adopted by, the local community. Although the Jews of Tunisia's *hara* (in Arabic, *harat al-yahud*, the Tunisian Jewish quarter) are represented in a handful of works by Danon as well as by some fellow AIU teachers, *Ninette* stands out for its departure from folklore, its staging of a female protagonist who speaks in her own voice, and its awareness of the internal politics of

MAP I. Colonial Tunisia, c. 1934. Source: Bill Nelson, 2016.

the Tunisian Jewish communities. These communities were divided both by class and by origin, with the wealthy *Grana* (Jews of Italian descent who had come to North Africa as early as the sixteenth century) wielding power and cultural capital, and the more modest *Twansa* (in Arabic, *Tawānisa*, Tunisian or "indigenous" Jews) eking out a living in the trades.[2]

In addition to its literary qualities, *Ninette of Sin Street* reveals the multi-sectarian, multilingual, and multiethnic world of early-twentieth-century Tunisia. This world also existed before the French invasion and annexation of Tunisia in 1881, of course, but it was in certain respects artificially stimulated, consolidated, and even divided by colonial rule.[3] The novella thus offers a lively soundtrack of a bygone North Africa that finds only faint echo in the contemporary moment. That it should prove surprising, in the early twenty-first century, that one of the first literary works in French to emerge from North Africa was written by an Ottoman Jewish transplant and should feature a poor, unwed sometime prostitute, a single mother from Sfax, suggests how much we still stand to learn from history and from the secrets of Sin Street.

Vitalis Danon and the Alliance Israélite Universelle (AIU): Jewish Education between the Ottoman Empire, France, and Tunisia

In 1881, France invaded and occupied Tunisia, quickly establishing a French protectorate over a country that had existed, for some three centuries, as a semiautonomous province of the Ottoman Empire. A crossroads of the Mediterranean, Tunisia was home to a majority Muslim population and an internally diverse Jewish community with ancient roots. It had also been settled by Christians of various origins, but especially from Italy; these Italian settlers outnumbered the French settler population for the duration of the Tunisian protectorate (1881–1956).[4]

In Tunisia, as elsewhere in colonial North Africa, French authorities imposed a "civilizing mission" on its subjects that forcibly opened the door to acculturation for both Muslim and Jewish subjects of the Tunisian bey. Yet, when it came to access to secular education and, particularly, to the enrollment of poor and rural children, the efforts of the AIU gave Tunisia's Jewish community an advantage over Tunisian Muslims. Founded in 1860 by members of the Franco-Jewish elite, the AIU sought to "regenerate" Mediterranean and Middle Eastern Jewish boys and girls by offering them a French-inspired, French-language education.[5] The organization established its first Tunisian school in 1878, several years before the French protectorate became a political reality. Given this earlier access to French-language instruction for Jews, it should come as no surprise that the first works of Francophone literature to emerge from Tunisia were written by Jews.

Vitalis Haim Danon (1897–1969) came of age in two provincial towns—Edirne [Adrianople], in the Ottoman Empire, and Sfax, Tunisia. These cities had no direct, or indeed predictable, relationship to one another, save for the fact that both were home to Jewish communities targeted for "regeneration" by the AIU. At the time of Danon's birth, Ottoman Edirne was situated at the meeting point of trading routes that linked the northern Balkans to the Aegean Sea and the Adriatic to Istanbul, the imperial capital, and was home to Muslims, Christians, and Jews. Edirne's Jewish community, like all those of southeastern Europe and Ottoman Anatolia, was comprised primarily of Ladino- (or Judeo-Spanish-) speaking Sephardim, descendants of the Jews and *conversos* (forced converts) who traced their ancestry to medieval Iberia, from which they had been expelled at the hands of the Inquisition during the fifteenth and sixteenth centuries.

Like so many Jewish boys of this milieu, Danon began his education in a traditional Jewish school, a *meldar*, where he would have been educated, largely by rote, in the Jewish canon. At age eleven, he began studies at the local AIU school in Edirne, which had opened four decades earlier, in 1867 (when the AIU itself was still a fledgling institution). Danon referred to his father as one of that city's first "AIU apprentices," who, according to his son, urged all five of his children to attend AIU schools and serve the organization.[6]

In southeastern Europe, as in North Africa, the AIU aimed to fight persecution and bring about the emancipation of Jews in countries where they were not yet citizens; even more importantly, it aspired to

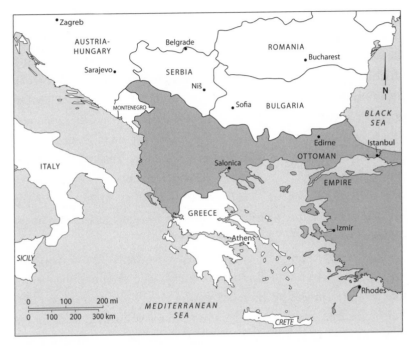

MAP 2. Major Ottoman Jewish centers of southeastern Europe, including Vitalis Danon's birthplace, Edirne, c. 1908. Source: Bill Nelson, 2016.

offer Levantine Jews an education in a bourgeois French mold. The organization's philosophical agenda emulated France's "civilizing mission" (*la mission civilisatrice*) toward its colonial subjects, but tinted it with a Jewish hue, brushing it, broadly and crudely, across the Mediterranean and Middle Eastern Jewish world. With the help of local Jewish communal leaders, the AIU was to open 183 schools by the eve of the First World War. In these classrooms, some 43,700 girls and boys received their first secular education (including the study of Jewish history and culture) in French. Over the decades that followed, the AIU encouraged generations of Sephardim to break with their past, offering them French as a new *lingua franca* for their social and cultural aspirations, along with the educational credentials to join a burgeoning, Europe-facing Mediterranean and Middle Eastern bourgeoisie.[7]

The most distinguished graduates of the AIU schools were selected by their teachers to take examinations to compete for enrollment in the AIU's teacher-training college in Paris, the École Normale Israélite Orientale. Danon couldn't have been much older than sixteen when he began studying at this institution. In the course of these studies, Danon became close to the director of the École Normale Israélite Orientale, Albert H. Navon, who apparently saw a budding literary talent in the young student. Danon was granted two degrees, a "Brevet Élémentaire" (the diploma required of all French elementary teachers) in 1914, and, in 1917, a "Brevet Supérieur," which was required of all AIU teachers.[8] (In 1924, he would add a "Certificat d'Aptitude Pédagogique" to this list of credentials.)

Danon's education in Paris coincided with the Balkan Wars (1912–1913), during which time Edirne was briefly conquered by Bulgaria before being recaptured by Turkey. After the First World War (1914–1918), Edirne became Greek according to the terms of the Treaty of Sèvres (1920). Fearing that this transition in rule would be attended by a rise in anti-Semitism, many of the city's Jewish residents fled, departing to settle abroad or to join larger Jewish communities elsewhere in the region. It is unclear whether Danon ever returned to his childhood home (which his parents, too, abandoned). In any case, the AIU intentionally and systematically assigned graduates of the École Normale Israélite Orientale to teach in schools distant from their childhood homes—in part to rupture their connection to the Judeo-Spanish spoken at home (whose use the AIU discouraged), but also to minimize distractions, including contact with family, that might take them away from their pedagogical work. Danon's first post was in Sfax, Tunisia. He traveled there for the first time (via Marseilles and Tunis) in the winter of 1917, scarcely twenty years old.

A minor Mediterranean port, which had for centuries been a vibrant regional hub of olive oil production, Sfax was a much smaller community than Danon's native Edirne. At the time of his arrival, it boasted a population of roughly twenty-eight thousand and a Jewish community of approximately twenty-six hundred.[9] In the era of the French Protectorate of Tunisia (1881–1956), many Tunisian Jews thrived, but at the moment that Danon arrived in Sfax, the local community was by and large poor and getting poorer, like the fictional Ninette. Among Danon's earliest letters from the city is one noting that Sfax had neither theater nor cinema. The young man found himself walking, and reading, a great deal.[10] Linguistic limitations surely hampered Danon in these early years—the Jews of Sfax, at that time, were more likely to speak Arabic than French. Indeed, Sfax's Jewish community was less international than that of Tunis, 270 kilometers to the north (or, for that matter, of Sousse, situated between Tunis and Sfax), where many Jewish middle- and upper-class families—some of whom had resided in Tunisia for generations—held foreign papers that afforded them advantageous trading conditions and freed them from certain local legal constraints. Most of the Jews of Sfax, on the other hand, as Danon wrote in a letter to his superiors in Paris, were "Tunisian Jews, subjects of the bey, and as such they fall under the jurisdiction of local courts."[11] To serve this community, the AIU opened both a boys' and a girls' school in 1905. At the time of Danon's arrival in the city, these remained the only secular schools for Jews in the city.

Of the many letters Danon would pen to the central offices of the AIU over some five decades, those of his early years in Tunisia are the most intimate and literary. With time, his correspondence would come to focus on quotidian concerns, especially the chronic underfunding of the AIU's schools in Tunisia. But in 1917, when he arrived in Sfax, Danon was stirred by all he encountered, very much under the spell of the AIU's philosophy, and (or at least so one suspects from his lengthy missives) lonely. These early letters, some of which are reproduced in this book's appendix, situate Danon as a flaneur dedicated to unpacking the mysteries of Tunisia's urban landscapes. North Africa was a novelty to Danon, and his reportage on its streets, smells, sights, and folkways freely recycled Orientalist tropes imbibed from the AIU curriculum.

Danon's letters, however, were not simply chronicles of the exotic. He expressed constant frustration at the AIU's underfunding of its schools in Sfax and at his meager salary, which was insufficient to cover the most

IMAGE I. Street scene, Sfax. Source: *Géographie pittoresque et monumentale des colonies françaises: Tunisie*. Paris: Flammarion, 1906, 155.

basic expenses and, initially, not even enough to cover the cost of a private room. Graver still, Danon was placed under a director he found unprofessional and irresponsible. Three and a half years after his arrival in Tunisia, Danon wrote the central offices of the AIU to proclaim that he would return to teaching only if the director was removed from service.[12] Danon returned to Europe in the fall of 1920—in time for the Jewish holidays— worried that he had permanently lost his "taste for the trade." The AIU must have placed great faith in its young apprentice, however, for the following year Danon was back at his post, the offending director removed.

Even before Danon's falling out with his superior, he had become engaged to an eighteen-year-old AIU pupil by the name of Fortunée Saban (1902–?). The Danons' first son, Roger Israel, was born in 1921, and the couple would go on to have three more children, a large family to support on the meager AIU salary that was, as Danon noted in a letter to his superiors, far less than it might have been had he married another AIU teacher (it was not uncommon for the AIU to place married teachers together).[13] On the occasion of the birth of his fourth child, Danon asked whether normal rules might be bent to allow him to eventually enroll his youngest in a local AIU school. This represented a violation of policy, as the AIU tended to subsidize the tuition of only three offspring per teacher, and Danon's request was indeed denied. Penury would haunt Danon throughout his service to the AIU, and, for that matter, thereafter. Immediately after his retirement in 1960, Danon initiated a long and complex plea to secure a more generous pension than he had been allocated.[14] While no longer a working teacher or school director, Danon still felt the sting of his employer's tightfistedness.

Notwithstanding these financial hardships, Danon remained loyal to the AIU for the entirety of his career. While many of his fellow AIU teachers were repeatedly relocated, Danon, remarkably, spent half a century in Tunisia. During this period, he served first in Sfax (1917–1921), then at the Hafsia school in the heart of Tunis's Jewish quarter (1921–1926). In 1926 he returned to Sfax and was promoted to director, a position he held for nearly twenty years. It was in Sfax that he lived through

IMAGE 2. Entry to Es-Nadli Street, Tunis. The street was an important tributary of Jewish life in Tunis. Circa 1950. Photo: Vitalis Danon. Source: Library of the Alliance Israélite Universelle (Paris).

the German occupation of Tunisia, a period made doubly anxious by the implementation of anti-Jewish measures (already instituted but not fully applied under the rule of the Vichy government) and the Allied bombing campaign that targeted Sfax—an Axis base and port and thus a strategic target—from November 1942 until its liberation by the British in April 1943. Although Danon and his family weathered the air raids from the relative safety of the countryside, he kept close tabs on the school in town and often travelled back to check on it. So deep was his commitment to the AIU school that upon one of his trips to Sfax—ostensibly a mission to save family belongings—he returned home having rescued desks and chairs from classrooms rather than heirlooms.[15] After the war, Danon returned to the Hafsia school to serve as director there (1945–1954), and from 1954 to 1958 he directed the Malta Srira school, a somewhat tonier establishment, also in Tunis. In 1954 Danon was also named director of all the AIU schools in Tunisia, a position he retained until his retirement in 1960, when he left Tunisia for good to settle in Cannes, France, where he died in 1969.

Perhaps it was the fact that his wife was Tunisian that made the country so attractive for Danon; perhaps it was his own immersion in the world of Tunisian letters (which we will describe in a moment); or perhaps, watching European geopolitics unfold from a distance, Danon felt ever less connected to his origins.[16] Small wonder that after the passage of the Morinaud Law of 1925 (which permitted Tunisian Jewish men to apply for French citizenship on an individual basis), Danon wrote with such sensitivity about how difficult it was for his Tunisian students to be denied the French citizenship granted their peers in neighboring Algeria, where most Jews had been granted citizenship by France by 1870.[17] Danon himself acquired French citizenship in 1925.

AIU policy dictated that before a new school was created, there needed to be an invitation from local Jewish leaders, and financial support for the schools tended to come from a combination of funds from the central AIU office in Paris, support from local notables and the community, and student tuition and fees. (The AIU's schools in Tunisia also

IMAGE 3. Jewish children in Gabès. Circa 1950. Photo: Vitalis Danon. Source: Library of the Alliance Israélite Universelle (Paris).

educated non-Jewish students: according to Danon, in 1931, twenty-five of the two hundred students in the boys' school in Sfax were Muslim.[18]) These were not easy alliances to maintain, and money was always scarce. In the late nineteen-twenties, Danon tried to edge into the olive oil market in order to raise money for the AIU school in Sfax. The results were ruinous and led him to ever more frantic fund-raising.[19] Danon was particularly irritated by his dependence on the Jewish community of Sfax because he perceived the community to be overly strict in religious practice and hence fundamentally ambivalent about the AIU's secularist agenda.[20] He was similarly frustrated by the local rabbi, who taught Danon's pupils Hebrew, as was common in AIU schools. Danon saw no reason why the rabbi should employ prayers as a tool of Hebrew pedagogy and implored him to adopt modern, secular methods of instruction instead.[21]

With time, Danon's own politics, including his views on Zionism, came to be influenced by the cultural and intellectual climate of Sfax. The city was particularly hospitable to Zionism. *Le Réveil Juif* (1924–1935), the most important Zionist newspaper in Tunisia, was based in Sfax in its early years, and in its pages the AIU was the object of vociferous critique.[22] Certain articles in this paper enraged Danon, who had begun his career as an opponent of Zionism, in the stalwart AIU tradition.[23] Danon's position towards Zionism would soften, however (as, in various respects, would the position of the AIU), and Danon eventually became a contributor to *Le Réveil Juif*, as well as to the short-lived *Cahiers du Bétar*.[24]

Some decades later, faced with the prospect of an independent, Arabophone Tunisia, Danon sought to persuade his AIU superiors to institute instruction in literary and dialectical Arabic in Tunisia. This innovation, Danon believed, would provide Jewish students with the tools required to participate in the new nation, all the while respecting the AIU's mission. At the same time, Danon ignored the national education imperatives that called for the suppression of Hebrew in favor of Arabic as a second language. Danon's desire to have it both ways—to continue to offer Hebrew-language instruction alongside lessons in Arabic—is emblematic of his impulse to put his students' needs before ideology. Moreover, it gives us insight into the tightrope act he performed on a daily basis, as he strove to uphold the AIU's goal of providing French education while inculcating modern Jewish principles and equipping his students with skills that would guarantee their ability to participate in the civic life of postcolonial Tunisia.

Danon's request was granted by his AIU superiors in 1956; the implementation of Arabic instruction, however, which allowed for just one hour per day of lessons in literary Arabic and which openly defied the reforms put in place by the newly created Tunisian National Ministry of Education, was likely not robust enough to have a significant impact. As elsewhere in the Mediterranean and Middle East, nationalizing efforts foretold the AIU's obsolescence, and the organization proved unable to recruit teachers equipped to instruct in the languages of the region's many new nation-states.[25] The swan song of the AIU would be sung in French. The pace of Jewish emigration from Tunisia increased in 1945 in the wake of the Second World War and accelerated with the country's declaration of independence in 1956 and the rise of Pan-Arabism, only to culminate in 1967 when, startled by the turn of events in the Middle East, most of the remaining Jews of Tunisia opted to leave. Yet the French-speaking Jewish world continued to thrive in diaspora, in the literature and culture of Tunisian Jews who gazed back at their homeland from France, Israel, and Canada. If Ninette once viewed Tunisian Jewish society from the gutter, the majority of Jews of Tunisian descent now view it through a lens both nostalgic and elegiac, from new homes abroad.[26]

A Local Literature in French: The Beginnings of the "Tunis School"

The acquisition of French—in North Africa as in the Middle East—was the linchpin of the AIU's philosophy; the ultimate goal was the emancipation and "regeneration" of Jews who were perceived, by members of the French elite, as backward. The French language was not seen as just an ordinary means of communication but was considered—by virtue of the supposed clarity and logic of its grammar— to have special properties of universality and reason.[27] But AIU students did not need to embrace these abstract principles in order to appreciate the social capital that fluency in French could offer them: for Jews in Tunisia it could provide, at least for a time, a pathway to citizenship through doors closed to the majority of Muslims, as well as serving as a tool for economic advancement.[28]

Geographically disparate, the AIU schools were nonetheless united by a common curriculum provided by the central committee in Paris, which established compulsory subjects and guidelines for hours of instruction. Irrespective of grade or gender (curricular norms for boys and girls were, in general, different), the minimum time devoted to "reading in French" and "French language" combined was always twice that of any other subject, including Hebrew, arithmetic, and "languages other than French."[29] If the opening of the first AIU school in Tunisia (in 1878) was a logical continuation of the AIU's commitments to North African Jews in general (the first AIU school was founded in Tetouan, Morocco, in 1862), by 1881, when Tunisia was declared a protectorate of France, educating the Jews of Tunisia in French had become a question of vital urgency.[30]

French was thus clearly an instrumental language, essential both to the AIU's abstract philosophy of moral regeneration and to practical concerns for Jewish economic survival within societies that were becoming increasingly more French-speaking and France-oriented. It was also, in the hands of AIU pupils-turned-instructors such as Danon, becoming a language of Jewish literary production. After his first short stint at the AIU school in Sfax (1919–1921), Danon was assigned to the Hafsia school in Tunis, in the heart of the *hara*. It was here that Danon became acquainted with Jacques Véhel and Ryvel, Tunisian Jews, fellow AIU instructors, and emerging chroniclers of the *hara*.[31] Danon's contact with Véhel and Ryvel seems to have been important for his own literary ambitions, for by the time he returned to Sfax to take up the directorship of the AIU school in 1926, he had published his first novel, *Le roman de la Manoubia* (The novel of Manoubia).[32]

If the five years in Tunis were critical for Danon's own literary ambitions, they were also foundational for Tunisian literature in French, for it was during their shared tenure at the Hafsia school (from 1921 to 1926) that Danon, Véhel, and Ryvel developed a common literary project, earning them the moniker "The Tunis School" (*l'école de Tunis*).[33] Individually and together—through co-authored projects such as *La hara conte: folklore judéo-tunisien* (The *hara* recounts: Judeo-Tunisian folklore) and *Le bestiaire du ghetto* (The ghetto bestiary)—these three men became the founding fathers not only of modern Judeo-Tunisian literature but of Francophone Tunisian literature more generally.[34]

The writings of the Tunis School gravitate towards themes of traditional Jewish life in Tunisia—a microcosm of society that was necessarily poor. While their vision of the *Twansa* (the Tunisian or "indigenous" Jews mentioned above) may have been accurate in certain respects, the Orientalist education of these writers likely influenced their tendency to frame the local Jews as an exotic and benighted population. The use of the expression "ghetto"—which the writers of the Tunis School employ interchangeably with "*hara*"—arguably transplants a medieval European concept to twentieth-century, colonial, and predominantly Muslim North Africa. Segregation, constraint, and marginalization are implicit in the term's history and etymology. The *haras* of Tunisia, however, like the mellahs of Morocco, were in fact porous and ethnically mixed neighborhoods, where (and through which) people of different religions and origins conducted commerce, socialized, and lived.[35]

It is this permeable, multicultural quarter that inspired *La hara conte*, an omnibus collection of seventeen short stories by the Tunis School writers. Personified in its ability to "recount," to tell its own stories, the Jewish quarter of these tales is full of "the children of Israel" but is also the territory of Bedouins, peasants, and soldiers.[36] The three authors approach their topic from different angles. Véhel's stories revisit age-old local myths and revive folkloric literary themes, such as the tale of la Kahéna, the Berber queen often called the North African Joan of Arc. Ryvel's contributions are grounded in the daily life of the *hara*, featuring episodes of rabbinic wisdom; healing rituals; coming-of-age stories; matchmaking; and tales of vice, petty crime, and justice. Whereas

Danon's pieces tend toward the essayistic and are anchored in his own observations, Véhel and Ryvel's tales are largely parables, their characters archetypes. All three writers liberally sprinkle their French with Judeo-Arabic expressions, which lends their prose a certain authenticity while implicitly nodding to a tradition of multilingualism.

While the subjects and poetics of *La hara conte* are emblematic of the Tunis School's agenda, the form of the *nouvelle*, or short story, is also significant insofar as it emerges as the genre par excellence for the representation of the Judeo-Tunisian condition.[37] In their desire to valorize local Jewish traditions while also demonstrating their own literary modernity, the authors walk a fine line. Choosing the short story meant calling upon both Arabic and Hebrew literary models—the *khurafa*, edifying tales in the tradition of *The Arabian Nights*, and stories told during Jewish gatherings—that were essentially oral, transmitted down through the generations.[38] The Tunis School writers conceived of themselves as mediators between what they might have called a retrograde Judeo-Arabic world, on the one hand, and a modern French world, on the other. Their bicultural status was both an ideological position and a marketing tool. In their authors' note at the end of *La hara conte*, they declare that "in bringing together these short stories we have not given in to the fleeting trend of Jewish novels written by half- or quarter-Jews, even by *goys*, who exploit this material and, by extension, us. All three of us were born and raised in Judaism; here, we gaze upon our brothers with kindness and love."[39]

Notwithstanding this unified front, Danon appears, in the stories written for *La hara conte*, to be already both distinguishing himself from his fellow writers and setting the stage for *Ninette de la rue du Péché: une nouvelle populiste*, the story that will be his last, and best-known, work of fiction. Of the seventeen short stories featured in the collection, only three are by Danon; and while "L'Adoption" (The adoption) is similar in content and tone to the pieces penned by Véhel and Ryvel, the other two by Danon—"Un enfant de la hara: récit d'un instituteur" (A child of the *hara*: a teacher's tale) and "Chez les Juifs de Djerba: notes de voyage" (On the Jews of Djerba: a travelogue)—are a stark departure from the folkloric fables and omniscient narration that characterize the collection overall. As AIU teachers, Véhel and Ryvel occupied an elite position in the Tunis Jewish community, yet they were nonetheless insiders. Steeped in the same local color that infuses their stories, they draw on a rich popular archive of anecdotes and archetypes. Although Danon was embraced by his Tunisian brethren, in his stories—particularly those in *La hara conte*—his position is that of what cultural anthropologists call "a participant observer," an individual who documents people, groups, and their interactions and surroundings while being fully immersed in the community. In "A child of the *hara*," for example, Danon describes his own encounter with the realities of life in the Jewish quarter and the impact of those conditions on his pupils' behavior. "On the Jews of Djerba" (a translation of which appears in the appendix) is a departure from the *hara*, as Danon narrates his trip to the island that boasts the oldest synagogue in Africa.[40] His disappointment at what he finds there speaks as much to the quasi-mythical status of the island in the Jewish imaginary as it does to the discomfiting realties of the place itself. Djerba, Danon surmises, is "a place that resists all civilization," (120) and yet upon departure he is gripped with emotion at having been welcomed "as a brother" (125). Not coincidentally, Djerba was the only Mediterranean Jewish community that refused to host an AIU school, which may have prejudiced AIU devotees against it.[41]

These early reflections nourished Danon's later writing, and in many ways *Ninette* can be read as the apotheosis of his literary project and perhaps of his own integration into the Judeo-Tunisian universe. In terms of genre, after *La hara conte* Danon began experimenting with the longer form of the novella—a genre faithful to the Tunis School model, yet long enough to do justice to the colorful life of Ninette.[42] Closer to the novel in length and in its ability to capture psychological complexities, the novella perhaps better reflected Danon's literary aspirations. Even as he strove to refine his art formally, he never lost sight of his subject—a care that is reflected in the book's original, vaguely ironic, subtitle "A populist novella." Thematically, *Ninette* is a distillation of Danon's observations of the *Twansa*. In it, we find descriptions of the Jewish quarter, of traditional beliefs and practices, and even of the "mythical" Djerbian Jew—all of which can be traced back to his earlier short stories. Some sources suggest that Ninette was in fact a real unwed mother in distress who found comfort in her son's education at the AIU. It is more likely, however, that she was a composite character whose story was derived from the many tales Danon heard in his role as director and the myriad real "characters"—students and parents alike—he encountered.

IMAGE 4. A young Jewish woman in Sfax. Source: *Géographie pittoresque et monumentale des colonies françaises: Tunisie*. Paris: Flammarion, 1906, 139.

By the time he arrived at *Ninette*, Danon had been in Tunisia for nearly twenty years, the last ten of which he had spent as the director of the AIU school in Sfax. He was the husband of a local woman and the father of four children. His education and professional status placed him amongst the elite, and his Ottoman origins would always make him a bit of an outsider, yet by 1938 Danon was sufficiently steeped in local culture to write an entire novella from the point of view and in the dialect of a destitute unwed mother and occasional prostitute, a local girl from "Sin Street." With *Ninette*, Danon had "gone native"—at least, in fiction.

Narrating *Ninette*: Gender and Politics in Provincial Tunisia

Ninette of Sin Street opens with the arrival of the titular protagonist at the AIU in the provincial town of Sfax. Acutely aware of the limited social mobility of early-twentieth-century colonial Tunisia, Ninette is not there for herself but on behalf of her young, illegitimate son, Israel, whose destiny she hopes to change through education: "Sign him up and teach him how to put ink on paper," she begs the director. "Make a man of him, not a know-it-all, nothing pie-in-the-sky, but a man who'll get me out of this mess I'm in." The "mess" in question is a life of abject poverty lived in the "ladies' quarter," or "Sin Street"—euphemisms for the zone on the edge of town to which prostitution is relegated—where Ninette cleans rooms and does laundry for a few coins, dreaming of "a little apartment on the Avenue (with) fine bed linens, and gowns, and draperies."

The first chapter, in which Ninette succeeds in convincing the AIU to enroll her son, establishes the tone and the structure for the remainder of the novella, which is organized into chapters corresponding to Ninette's successive visits to the AIU director over the course of six years, ostensibly to check on Israel's progress. Both the passage of time and the presence of the director as interlocutor are evident in the direct address that opens each visit/chapter: "Mr. Director, Sir, it's Ninette again. Good day to you, first of all"; "Six months since you last saw me, really? How time flies, doesn't it?" For nearly the entire novella, the director doesn't speak at all; his existence is implied through apostrophe, lending the text a confessional or talk-therapy quality as Ninette narrates episodes from her past in stream-of-consciousness monologues. With her colorful local patois, complete with colloquial borrowings from Jewish scripture, idiomatic grammar, and words or expressions from Italian and Arabic, the novella is a stylistic and linguistic celebration of the vernacular that paints a vivid and sometimes humorous slice-of-life portrait of what might otherwise be a tragic tale of poverty, abuse, and forced prostitution.

Ninette is the natural heir to the traditions established by the early Tunis School stories, yet while the tale remains true to the socioeconomic realities it seeks to depict, Danon's novella departs from traditional representations, particularly in its handling of gender and space. An AIU teacher's discovery of the *hara* and of the poverty of his students was a recurrent motif for the Tunis School writers, generally narrated by the teacher and describing his first encounter with the ghetto and its conditions.[43] In *Ninette*, the situation is reversed: it is she, the poor Jew, who leaves the *hara* and Sin Street to go to the school and talk with the director. Moreover, one can't help but notice that Ninette is an extremely mobile character. While her narration takes place at the school, in the safe confines of the director's office, the story she tells is a peripatetic one, as circumstances take her from Sfax to the capital and back again.

If it is remarkable to find an itinerant female protagonist in early Judeo-Tunisian literature, it is equally significant to encounter such a chatty one. Danon gives Ninette both physical and narrative agency. Her ability to "think on her feet" (to pick up and leave when situations go bad; to find help when she needs it) is doubled by her capacity to "think out loud," to narrate all of these adventures and, in so doing, to reflect on them and give them meaning. It isn't long before the reader starts to hear Ninette's voice in her mind and identify her storytelling strategies and linguistic tics: her tendency to minimize her own suffering and to cloak her sexual adventures and misadventures in euphemism; her ample use of colorful metaphor; her tendency to misquote—or strategically reformulate—scripture; and her uncanny knack for questioning religious tenets while appearing wondrously naïve.

IMAGE 5. Young Jewish woman and child en route to the communal oven in Gabès. 1950. Photo: Vitalis Danon. Source: Library of the Alliance Israélite Universelle (Paris).

To have given this sort of leading role to an indigenous Jewish woman, a sometime prostitute no less, and to have done so successfully and with such poignancy, is noteworthy, and we would be remiss in not reminding a twenty-first-century reader that this type of gender representation—and the degree of agency shown by Ninette—was rare in early-twentieth-century North African literature. Ninette's ultimate ability to turn away from prostitution (despite its lure of "easy" money) and the good sense she displays by investing in her son's education do not just provide a happy ending. These changes suggest that the downtrodden can raise themselves up and that women—historically and culturally disenfranchised—can improve their lot. Ninette's situation at the end of her tale suggests that one's fate might not be predestined by biology, gender, religion, or economic status.

At the same time, it is impossible to ignore the fact that Ninette is Danon's fictional construct, and readers must be wary of the suitability of feminist interpretation. Her stream-of-consciousness narrative comes to an abrupt end when the silent director (Danon's mouthpiece) decides to speak, in the novella's very last scene. Ninette's story finishes on a high note—she has plans to move out of Sin Street and into a respectable apartment on a grand avenue—but the intrusion of the director-Danon compels us to weave the author back into our understanding of the text. It is the director, not Ninette, who has the literal last word, and his words are nothing less than a benediction:

> Ninette, didn't I tell you that sooner or later, all your grief would be rewarded in this life? . . . Well done, Ninette. You and your son have put the worst behind you now. Pain, sorrow, shame, all that can be forgotten. And like good folks who love each other, you can move forward into a bright future. And look! There's a little sunshine just come out to brighten and warm your way. Good luck, Ninette, good luck! (84)

Ninette and her son Israel now benefit from an "illumination" that is both literal ("a little sunshine") and ideological, as the director preaches the AIU rhetoric of European enlightenment, French Republican idealism, the belief in the perfectibility of man, and the promise of the civilizing mission.[44] Danon's "nice little sunshine" refers to Israel's educational success (whose natural byproduct is a situation of respectability for Ninette herself), to the warm glow of civilization emanating from Alliance ideology, and to the triumph of morality evidenced by Ninette's ability to be no longer "of Sin Street." The conclusion, then, leverages imagery of literal enlightenment to signify deeper meaning: the triumph of knowledge over ignorance, of civility over barbarism, and of moral Europe over the putatively immoral Orient.

Ninette of Sin Street ends well for the title character and her son, and it would take a coldhearted reader to begrudge Ninette her incremental step up the social ladder. Yet the happy ending forces us to wonder whether Ninette really ever had a voice at all and to review the text in the light of Danon, who inserts himself—as AIU school director—into this morality tale. It becomes clear by the end that the novella is, in addition to its other various qualities, also a rousing chorus of AIU propaganda. Ninette's status as a sometime prostitute is essential to this. For the good works of the Alliance to attain their full symbolic value as morally curative and for the novella to function as a propaganda vehicle, it would not suffice for Ninette to be an ordinary downtrodden indigenous Jew—poverty, after all, is not immoral. However, by making Ninette not only a prostitute but a woman born into prostitution, Danon suggests that immorality may be as much a question of nature as nurture, a predisposition exacerbated by circumstance and environment.[45]

Even as we may bristle at this vision of Ninette—is she nothing other than the savage saved by civilization, the symbol of the triumph of West over East, reason over sorcery, modernity over tradition, civilization over indigeneity?—we note that Danon has not only made her an archetype but has given her a certain critical spirit. Like so many other heroes and antiheroes of modern Jewish literature, Ninette embeds, in her earnest comments, pointed critiques of religion and the rabbinate. Ninette's continual "mistakes" in quoting scripture might be read as evidence of her lack of education.[46] But these moments might also be taken as Danon's demonstration of the religious elite's failure to speak the language of its flock—or, indeed, to grant girls access to religious education. And of course, it is the rabbi from Djerba who lands Ninette the job that is her final undoing and then fails to help her when she ends up pregnant. With *Ninette*, Danon comes into his own not only as an observer of the Tunisian Jews but as their representative—in senses both political and aesthetic. He is their champion, their emissary, and their defender. Ninette's story is, after all, as much *his* story as it is hers; in it, the success of the AIU mission is manifested through upward mobility, narrative mastery, and this outsider who manages to imagine himself an insider.

From "La rue du Péché" to "Sin Street": Issues of Translation

The challenges of translating any work of literature have as much to do with context as with linguistic systems, and all translators face a series of decisions about precisely how much to "localize"—that is, make accessible to readers of the target language—references to cultural phenomena. With *Ninette*, translating the now dated vernacular of the protagonist is made more challenging by virtue of the already polyglot environment of the Jews of Tunisia and of Ninette's own idiosyncratic use of French. After all, it is likely that Danon's rendition of this quasi-monologue is already a form of translation itself, as a poor, uneducated Tunisian Jew would have more readily spoken Judeo-Arabic than French. Rather than transpose the verbal twists and turns of *Ninette* to an analogous Anglophone environment (a former British colony, for example, or even the antebellum American south), we the editors, in consultation with our translator, have opted to retain, to the degree that it was possible, Ninette's Tunisian-ness. In the able hands of Jane Kuntz, the English translation lets the original multilingualism shine through.

This strategy entails allowing Ninette to continue to use the colorful Italian and Arabic expressions that mark her speech in French as especially sited in provincial, colonial Tunisia and its porous Jewish quarters. When Ninette uses an Italian expression such as *la robba vecchia* (an Italian expression for "old clothes" that was commonly used in Tunisia), we have retained the Italian in the English translation and added a note for reader comprehension. Similarly, we have opted to keep Arabic words that refer to local foods and customs, not simply because they add authenticity to the English text (this is the case for *boukha*, a Tunisian fig brandy) but also because their denotative meanings often have important metaphorical consequences. Thus, when Ninette announces that it was all "a big *chakchouka* in my head," she is referring not only to a particular egg dish where many ingredients are tossed together, but to her own state of confusion, a lack of mental clarity, a situation in which her mind is "scrambled."

In the various stories and anecdotes she relates, Ninette also calls upon lines from the Torah, usually paraphrasing a story her rabbi has recounted. This particular form of intertextuality is delicate, as Ninette often misquotes or simply vernacularizes both familiar and more esoteric passages of scripture. It was important to us not to "correct" Ninette's versions, even in cases where the original source might not be transparent. After all, not only would a correction change the very essence of *Ninette*, but it would also undermine the subtle critiques of religion and the rabbinate that are couched in these occasionally comic misappropriations. Ninette in English thus makes analogous, vaguely mocking missteps in her citations.

Finally, the English retains the highly oral flavor of this text, giving our Anglophone Ninette the same chatty, vernacular sparkle that won over the AIU director.

After Ninette and Danon

Almost a century after the Tunis School writers penned their first portraits of the *hara*, the subjects that inspired their folkloric, ethnographic novellas have all but vanished from North Africa. It would be wrong to say that there are no more Ninettes in Tunisia at all—the archetype may live on with variations on the theme—but the statement is nevertheless not so far from the truth. The Sin Streets of contemporary Tunisia no longer house *Twansa*, Arab, and Italian "ladies" down on their luck. Indeed, after the 2011 ouster of President Zine al-Abadine Ben Ali (which brought with it a wave of largely tolerated Salafism), the brothels and red-light districts of Sfax, Sousse, and Kairouan were closed. However, the example of Abdellah Guech—the historical red-light district of the capital, situated in the medina just steps from the Zeitouna Mosque—is instructive. Once a space where both workers and their clientele were multicultural and multilingual, Abdallah Guech has evolved apace with greater Tunisian society: its sex workers, nearly all of whom are Muslim Tunisians, are now registered "employees of the state" and, out of deference to sensibilities, the district is closed to business on the holy days of Friday and Saturday—but only during Ramadan.

Yet the story of Tunisia's Ninettes and their destiny is perhaps more potently yoked to the story of Tunisian Jewry in the twentieth century. One hundred and five thousand strong in 1945, the Jewish community of Tunisia had been reduced, by the beginning of the twenty-first century, to some two thousand souls, nearly half of whom resided on the island of Djerba. Between 1948 and the mid-nineteen-fifties—following the experience of German occupation and the promulgation of France's anti-Semitic Vichy laws in 1942–1943, and fearful that the rising tide of pro-independence sentiment would spell difficulty for non-Muslims— twenty-five thousand Tunisian Jews left their country. By the end of the nineteen-sixties, and as a result of the Six-Day War that pitted Israel against Egypt, Jordan, and Syria and spurred anti-Jewish riots in Tunisia, nearly all the remaining Jews had left, trading their native land for exile in France, Canada, or Israel.[47] Many Jews of Tunisian origin or descent have since continued to visit Tunisia and to maintain friendships, property, and business ties there. Still, Tunisia's permanent Jewish community is now minuscule relative to what it once was.

Danon himself resettled his family in France in 1960, when he retired from the AIU after a forty-year career. The timing of his decision to leave, four years after Tunisian independence, fits imperfectly with the main waves of emigration. While a figure such as Albert Memmi (Tunisia's most celebrated writer and a product of AIU schooling) left for

France immediately after decolonization in 1956—citing the foreclosure of opportunities for Jews in the newly independent Muslim-majority nation—Danon remained.[48] We might read Danon's comparatively deferred departure as symbolic of his abiding dedication to educating the Jews of Tunisia. Given his passionate belief in the mission of the AIU, it is impossible not to wonder whether he delayed his departure because he was waiting to confirm that there was truly nothing more he could do.

We would do well to remember Danon and Ninette not as nostalgic symbols of a bygone multiculturalism but as potent examples of just how recently the streets of Tunisia bustled with people of myriad ethnic and religious origins, whose problems were perhaps not so different from theirs. More generally, however, the novella reminds us that today's divisions were yesterday's combinations. Ninette, both an Arab and a Jew, embodies what some may view as a contradictory identity, and yet her

IMAGE 6. A class from the Hafsia School of the Alliance Israélite Universelle, Tunis, visits an exhibit celebrating the history of the AIU. Pictured are 3 AIU teachers: Joseph Lévy, Vitalis Danon, and Ange Hattab (from left to right). April 1958. Source: Library of the Alliance Israélite Universelle (Paris).

concerns point away from the political and the ideological toward the pragmatic, the quotidian, even the elemental: she wants a safe place to sleep, a better life for her son, a bit of respectability. If the lessons of Sin Street are grounded in a set of circumstances that belong to an erstwhile colonial moment, they nonetheless speak to these human needs, to concerns that transcend any particular time and place.

Lia Brozgal and Sarah Abrevaya Stein

Ninette of Sin Street

by Vitalis Danon

I

Morning, Mr. Director, Sir. Well, here I am, it's me, Ninette. Which one, you ask?

I guess there *are* quite a few of us in this town, aren't there!

Well, since you asked, I'm the Ninette who lives over that way, as you walk up toward the city walls, and you land right in the middle of the . . . well, you know . . . the "ladies' quarter," Sin Street, with all due respect.

A room in town? Heavens no, I could never afford that, not in this life, anyway. Money's what you need for that. And with the chump change I earn working for the rich—thirty, forty, all right let's say fifty centimes in good times—I can just about keep bread on the table for my little boy. So, you see, I can't be too choosy. I take what lodgings I can get, a little hole in the wall over by the . . . "ladies," who aren't worse than anyone else, mind you, since they do help us through bad times. A small room to clean here, a little laundry there, some errands, I can always earn a few coins off them, too.

Trouble is, my little boy here isn't so little anymore and is starting to figure things out. You see, all day long, we get Senegalese infantrymen, Algerian cavalrymen, Arabs, Bedouins, Maltese, Jews, Greeks, or Sicilians, who come and go, look over the merchandise before picking one out to take into a back room and have a go.

Everyone said: take your son to the Jewish school! So here I am. You'll take him, of course, won't you? They wouldn't have him anywhere else since he doesn't have the papers, you see. You know, birth certificates, that sort of thing. Where do you think I can get them? The kid's got no father: I was dumped as soon as I confessed there was a little one on the way. No offense meant, Sir, but it's the honest truth. No sense hiding it, everybody knows. So, you understand the tricky situation I'm in at present. But I do know that he's mine, isn't that right, my little Israel? Look at him, will you? All nice and clean. So you'll take him, right? You can't go and turn me out like the others have, can you? You'll sign him up, right? What's that bit of paper everyone's asking for anyway? Something that important, wouldn't the Creator have tacked that on when he made us?

My son's name, you ask? I just said it, didn't I? Israel. Israel what? How am I supposed to know? You're cleverer than me: what do you call a kid who's missing a father?

As for me, I'm Ninette, the one and only. You haven't heard of me, really? Well, how can that be? Maybe it's because you're not from these parts. Or you look the other way when your nasty little charges are pelting me with stones when school lets out. You've never seen the way they corner me, then grope and pinch until I'm black and blue? Just for laughs, they say, just for jollies. Come on, I know what men are all about. Pigs, the lot of them, save one or two. They get all excited seeing me on my back like that, arms and legs flailing. Very sorry, Sir, I don't mean to annoy you. Oh, come on, do a girl a favor and take my son in. Don't go and send him away for something so silly. Sign him up and teach him how to put ink on paper. Make a man of him: he doesn't have to be a genius—I'm not that ambitious—but a man who'll get me out of this mess I'm in.

Look at me, I'm only twenty-six, but I've been working for the last fifteen of those years, doing this and that. And underpaid, and scolded, and beaten, oh yes, kicked in the behind; and fed in the kitchen where the lady of the house has me eat along with her cats!

Who wouldn't be this spiteful and hateful, when year in and year out, day and night, you're doing nothing but washing, scrubbing, rinsing, polishing, ironing, mending, cooking special little dishes for Madame— she's got a delicate stomach, poor thing—and for Monsieur, who stuffs himself . . . ?

All right, all right, I'll hold my tongue. That's what happens when I get angry. They're right to slap me around. They have to beat some sense into me somehow, don't they? I'm like fresh octopus: the harder you hit them, the tenderer they get.

So, it's done then, you'll sign him up, my son. And I'll be off, happier than when I came, that's for sure. And I'll be thinking to myself on the way: Ninette, old girl, you're a fool—always been one, in fact— that much is clear. But that doesn't mean your son has to be one. You'll wear yourself out for years to put your son through school, to dress and feed him. And if that means taking hard-earned bread out of your own mouth, then so be it. You'll be doing it for him. And you'll show the world that Ninette can do things right when she sets her mind to it.

Ah, my son! When he's all grown up and earning a living, there won't be a mother on earth prouder than me. We'll stroll arm-in-arm around the bandstand, when the fine ladies strut by in their feathered hats with their la-di-da airs, with their busts and bustles all rustling in silk. And my son will pat me on the hand and say: don't worry, Mama, I'm rich, let's go to the shops and buy whatever we want.

So off we'll go window-shopping, and pick out a few things, though he says nothing there is good enough for me, dear boy.

And fine bed linens, and gowns, and draperies, we'll buy them all by the dozen, by the bolt. And jewelry for me, pearls and diamonds. And a thousand francs, and then another thousand he puts into my purse, saying: here Mama, take this and give it out to the poor. And when it's all gone, there'll always be more, don't forget.

That's what my son's going to be, that's what he'll be saying some day.

Oh, but don't look at me now, with my torn skirt, my faded scarf, my bare feet in secondhand slippers from the *robba vecchia*!* Money's round; it rolls. One day to you, another day to me, and on it goes. What makes you think it wouldn't make a stop at my door one day and brighten up my life a bit? Don't you think old Ninette has earned herself a little attention from the Almighty? Hasn't she? Never hurt anyone in my life, have I, not even a fly, folks will tell you as much. Always wanted good, never evil. It's just that the good wanted nothing to do with me, so it was evil that came along instead.

So there he is, Sir. I'm putting him in your hands, my little one.

He's the apple of my eye, he is. He's not a bad boy, you'll see. He's just too scared, that's all. He's been beaten about so much by me and everyone else that he raises an elbow for cover as soon as anyone comes close. And he shakes, good Lord how he shakes! After giving him a good walloping, I'm always on my knees begging for forgiveness, hugging and kissing him and crying my eyes out. I roll on the ground like a kitten to let him stomp all over me.

That's my boy, my little man, the love of my heart. But he's the enemy, too, living proof of my shame and the wickedness of some man.

You've the patience of Job, to hear me out like this. Send me away! Come on, send me away already! We'll be here all night, otherwise, all year even, until the end of the world . . .

I'm a chatterbox, don't mind me. Once I open my mouth, there's no shutting me up!

So good day to you, Sir. I'm back to my pots and pans now. Have to keep living, whether your heart's full of cares and woe, or singing like a bird.

Get a move on, Ninette. Keep on going till you get to the other side, where there's no more shame or grief, no more birth certificates or bastards, or anything. We're all the same, my lovely ladies, all a feast for worms, with a clump of earth for a pillow and a nice-sized stone on the

---

* *robba vecchia*: Italian for "old dresses or clothing," this was a phrase used by rag peddlers in Tunisia who went house to house collecting old clothes or other items for resale.

belly. Yes, ladies and gentlemen, it's just like I say, like what the rabbi reads at the synagogue. You haven't heard him? You might go have a listen some day. My oh my, what you'll learn about what's waiting for you over there! It'll make you think twice before messing around, since we're all going to end up *kif-kif*,* big and small, nasty and kindhearted, the do-nothings and the have-nothings, even the fellow tooling around in his automobile. That's a consolation, old girl, and not the least.

See you next time, Sir, alive and well. If it's all right with you, Ninette will be stopping by from time to time after class, to see how the little one is doing.

And especially, if you please Sir, don't ask me any questions, all right? There have been such unspeakable things in my life! I don't really care so much, I'm just plain old me. I don't hold anything back. But you, Sir, I wonder how you can listen to an unwed mother who lives on Sin Street?

II

Morning to you, Sir. It's me again, Ninette.

It's been some months, hasn't it? How are you doing, first of all?

Thank you for my son, too. You're really spoiling him, with a slate, colored crayons, the whole deal, eh?

Me? Same as always. Have to get by with what you've got, right? I laugh, I cry, I pout, I moan and groan about everyone and everything, and then I just get on with it.

Don't you laugh at me, now! Sometimes I say to myself: Ninette, I say, if I were the Almighty—just supposing, right?—or something like that, I would send some huge disaster to the world. And then, we'd start all over.

But it seems, according to the rabbi, that he already tried that once, and it didn't work out so well. A shame, isn't it? So now, to keep us waiting, they're promising us a Messiah.

Do you believe in the Messiah, you Sir?

---

* *kif-kif*: this is an expression that originated in North African Arabic and has been used in French since the nineteenth century; it indicates "the same" or "equal."

Saturday's my day off, so I take my little son by the hand and we're off to the synagogue to hear the rabbi. He's this fellow from Djerba with a big moustache that takes up half his face, and a black beard so long it's endless.* But he knows his stuff, no question about it, and he's a good speaker. He says the Almighty is watching over everything and everybody (me included! though you'd never know).

So, later on, much later on, in I don't know how many years, I won't be doing laundry anymore; no more of this backbreaking work for me, running around from dawn to dusk for a crust of bread and a couple raw onions for my sonny and me.

He puts it like this: the more problems we have down in this world, the better things will be later, up there in the other. Take me, for example: wretch that I am, dumped by my son's father, I'll be sitting on a golden throne up there, in a house full of carpets, carpets on every floor. And in the streets, flowers everywhere and greenery, instead of all that stinking filth.

No more need to go to the public fountain and fight over whose turn it is, water will spring up from the ground and flow as pure as diamonds.

That's what the rabbi from Djerba says.

You should see this rabbi's clientele—beggars, old folks, the para- lyzed, the drunk, the blind—and how they stare wide-eyed when he says those things! They're so spellbound, in fact, that they fall asleep and snore through the rest of the service, poor devils.

I feel lulled too, at first. But then I realize: this flea-bitten cleric is also filling my mind with notions as intoxicating as the fig *boukha*† of his homeland!

I come to my senses, filled with rage: enough! Enough lies! It's a sin to

---

* Home to an ancient community of Jews, the island of Djerba was a rich source of religious and spiritual inspiration for Tunisian Jewry as a whole (see also the introduction to this book). In a 1937 letter to his superiors at the Alliance Israélite Universelle in Paris, Danon described Djerba as "the fortress, the refuge for the Torah . . . where tradition is still respected in its purest form like nowhere else." AIU XII.E.50b, "Danon, 1933," letter by Vitalis Danon to the president of the AIU, 24 September 1937.

† *boukha*: this Tunisian alcoholic beverage, an eau-de-vie made out of figs, originated in Djerba and was traditionally manufactured by Jewish families. Alcohol does not carry the same prohibi- tion among Jews as among Muslims.

lead poor folks on like that. Your tales are taller than your beard is long! If it's true, what you're saying, and I mean God's truth, then give me just a little bit of it right now. Waiting around like this, mouth open, I can't take it anymore, I'm at the end of my rope.

Take yesterday, for instance. I did a huge load of laundry for Stitra Perez. That evening, she puts a few miserable coins in my hand. They work us to the bone, and then they wonder why the Messiah isn't coming . . .

From there, I went to the butcher's shop.

Messaoud the butcher, what a despicable person! He looks down on you like he's second cousin to the bey or something. He's got meanness oozing from every pore of that yellow face of his.

"So Ninette," he says, "what'll it be for you today? A leg of lamb or a pound of chops? Shall I remove some of the fat for you?"

His steely gaze lights up and his moustache curls like a cat's, trying not to laugh.

And I think to myself: go ahead, make fun all you want. Ninette may be standing in front of you, but Ninette isn't here. Her mind is somewhere else; she's not listening. She's trying to figure out how she's going to pay for food and rent with the pittance she's just received.

You give a franc to the landlord, and you are already poorer by half. Then you get some pasta for five centimes, two more for tomato sauce, with the rest going to the butcher. We'll see what you can get from him. A bone, that's all. And even then, if there's a little marrow in it, wouldn't that be nice?

But, as if it wasn't enough that I'm a hardship case, he makes things worse by suggesting cuts that I couldn't afford if I saved a year's wages!

Another one who quickly paid for all the harm he did.

Starved us, he did, sold us bones instead of meat, poor wretches that we were! Bones they wouldn't even give to dogs! He began lending money here and there, by the hundreds, then the thousands. Those hundreds and thousands vanished. You just try running after them now, you old fool. And you let me know when you catch anyone.

Like I said, as long as there's that kind of scum around, the Messiah will be too disgusted to show up.

But those of us who live in the hope of a better life where it's not so cold and we'll eat our fill, what's to become of us, then?

Between me and other folks, there's a—how to put it?—a kind of wall I keep running into. Even the worst-paid housecleaning jobs, I can't even get those anymore.

Folks are afraid of me, they avoid me, turn me away! As if I still had the heart to joke around, as if I wasn't completely nauseated by now at the thought of . . . , well, you know what.

I look like a sick cat, eyes all washed out from crying so much, chest as flat as a pancake and legs like a knock-kneed mare. So you know of a fellow who'd want—what do I mean, *want*? Let's not be pretentious— who'd so much as look at me?

But I'm thinking deep down: look, Ninette, you've never tied the knot, and yet you're a mother. How is that? Not the way it's supposed to be. So go hang yourself. Then, you have a kid who's not like other kids, declared, registered, written into the books with his special serial number, tags and collar—like dogs and automobiles registered at City Hall. No, he's not the way he's supposed to be. So go hang yourself for that, too.

And then, what about your own birth, the way you came into the world? Was that the way it was supposed to be? Well, to start out with, you came crashing down out of nowhere like a catastrophe. To think that you were exactly eleven days old when your mother died of childbed fever. And on day twenty, your old dad kicks the bucket, too. Tell me, now, Ninette, whether that's an ordinary way to grow up in a family.

Grandma—may she rest in peace wherever she is—used to say: Ninette, I don't mean to make you feel bad, but for sure you were born under an unlucky star.

Fine. If the stars start meddling, then there's nothing to be done, is there? Too bad they're hung so high up there, where we can't at least spit in their faces and tell them they're meaner than measles, to be going after a wretch like me.

Sometimes I believe what the rabbi says—that it's the Almighty that does everything—and sometimes I don't believe a word of it. And anyway, he—the Almighty, I mean—must be stronger than the stars, right? For example, my unlucky star should've given me an even harder time. Well, it didn't! With no father or mother, nothing except what care my grandma could provide, I survived and grew. Now there's a miracle for you! Yes, that poor old lady went from house to house begging a breastfeeding for me, a crust of bread for herself. And the women gave what they could so that the cries of the thirsty little bundle wouldn't bring bad luck to their own nurslings.

There was one in particular, an Italian lady, our neighbor on Sin Street. Abandoned by her lover who had left her with child, she began taking in clients just like the other wretches were doing. No one was casting the first stone. How else could we eat, put clothes on our backs, and pay for our rooms?

So her little one had just been weaned when I arrived on the scene. But still, morning and afternoon, she would come knocking at our door, and in her half-Arabic, half-Italian, would ask for me so that she could give Allah's share, as she used to say.

Pretty nice nursery, I have to say, this Sin Street where I grew up, where I would be rocked to sleep by the obscene songs of infantryman lodgers.

Oh, you shouldn't sound so surprised, Sir! There's not one, but ten or twenty of your pupils that live on Sin Street and the neighborhood. What do you expect? They're too poor to afford a room in town. You should see them, right at sundown, how they rush home and huddle in their closet-sized quarters, out of fear of passersby and prowlers. This is where all the drunks and bad boys hang out. And whenever something ugly happens, it's the cop who's the first to get out of there. Clean up your own messes, he says.

What do you think, Sir? Isn't it worse than murder, exposing these good families to vice all out in the open like that?

Nobody wants to defend us, since we're just nobodies from nowhere. No one gives a damn. We've been living like this for years now, and they'll let us go on living in the same filth. And if you kick up a fuss about it, there'll be hell to pay. They'll call you an anarchist, a communist, or who knows what else! And you'll end up in the slammer, because you supposedly wanted to set the town on fire.

As far as I'm concerned, no need to wait for the urban master plan, or the mister plan, or whatever, from City Hall. Might as well just wait for the Messiah while you're at it. So I made a resolution, and here it is: I'm going to get myself out of here, and move my stuff into a little apartment on the avenue, you know which one, with the palm trees and the statue in the square. That's where I'll be living, you see if I won't. Just wait until my son gets his certificate. And we'll see what's what.

When he's all grown up and educated and all, my son, this is what I'll tell him: I'll say look, here's what we've been suffering all these years, and why. So first, you'll give an order so that if a woman comes and says "sign up my son," the clerk working for the Big Man won't have the right to ask who she had the kid with, or where's the husband. And if he's impolite enough to ask, they'll shut him up with: I had the kid with God Almighty, get it?

And that's the sort of lessons I'll give him. Son, I'll say, don't you remember when we were poor and lived on Sin Street?

Don't you remember the Greek sailors, the Sicilians, the *spahis** that used to knock at our door, and we would shout from inside: move on, we're a clean family here!

Don't you remember that time they killed Marietta—you remember, that beautiful woman who used to give you candy and kisses—and it was some Greek who stabbed her? The whole neighborhood was up in arms that night!

Don't you remember when I used to stuff cotton in your ears, and you'd say: but Mama, I don't have an earache! And I'd say: oh yes you do!

Silly boy, it was to keep you from hearing the dirty songs out in the streets, the swearing, the insults, the catcalls for the ladies, the gunshots.

---

* Derived from an Ottoman term, *spahi* refers to a North African Arab or Berber who served in the French cavalry, representing France locally and overseas.

And don't you remember this, and that, and that other thing?

Don't you remember?

Ah, my boy! Kids shouldn't have to have memories like the ones you have. Do what you have to, whatever it takes. Give your whole fortune, even your life, to keep good and evil apart!

That's what I'll tell my son later on.

You see, Sir, if what happened to me happened, it's because we were cheek by jowl with vice all of the time.

You want to know *what*, Sir? Well . . . , let's leave that for next time. That's all I'm going to say for today.

The rabbi, he explains it fancy-like: "Every hour has its own suffering," I think it goes. Which means, Ninette, don't try to lift more than you can carry.

As for the load I'm carrying today, it's a heavy one, so heavy that I don't even feel like dragging it all the way home.

But I have to think of my little puppy of a boy who's already waiting for me at the door.

So there it is, I have to keep living and hoping for his sake. Yes, that's very true, what you just said, Sir: if you take hope away from the desperate, what do they have left?

Hope's cheap, say those who have everything they want. It's a fool's consolation, they also say.

Fine, I'll be a fool, then; but don't take away my hope.

III

So, what's new, Mr. Director Sir? Been a while now that I've been saying to myself: Ninette, you shouldn't be impolite. Go over and say hello to your son's teacher. He's not like all the others, all snooty and scornful. He'll listen even when you're telling him uninteresting stuff. Doesn't cut you off, just lets you unwind your chatty ball of string.

That's what I've been thinking to myself for some time.

So today, you won't stop me from thanking you. For what, you ask? For what? You've forgotten, then. What about the honorability certificate you gave my son? Now, don't go and act all surprised. Oh, I get it. I know you call it the honor roll, but I'm stubborn about certain things, and I call it the honorability certificate, and that's all there is to it.

Don't you think I'm right, Sir?

Because my son doesn't have a proper father, people look at us like we're some kind of separate species. Something like animals that don't deserve any pity or consideration. When it comes to pity, they can keep it, I don't care. But consideration, that's what I want. I know it's not food on the table, but it sure helps keep your spirits up in bad times. Something you can't do without, I mean it.

So, when the kid came home with this beautiful piece of paper, all written out in big gold letters: "Israel, son of Ninette, for his fine work and good conduct," everybody in the neighborhood came out to see it, the Djerbian grocer, the water carrier, all the neighbors, the women who service the soldiers, and the ones who handle those city slickers in flared trousers, everybody wanted to have a look. People grabbed at it like it was some kind of wonder. My son's honor became everyone else's, too.

Hey, dummy, they said to him. Wipe your nose and get over here, so we can congratulate you and your mother.

And one of the women added: come over here and let me see. It's not because he's Ninette's son, or that he's not as good as other kids. It's not because we work this lousy job that we're less honorable. The boy is ours, we're the ones who raised him, and raised his mother too, for that matter.

She continued: bravo, Ninette. We could use a half-dozen or so of boys like yours. Give us a kiss, old girl, and don't worry. You're on the right path now, you'll get out of here someday. Go on, leave us where we are, and follow your destiny!

So there you have it, Sir. And that night, they wanted to drag me out and drink to my son's little diploma, to celebrate properly, at Panayotti's place, the one that keeps the whole neighborhood supplied with wine.

But I refused flat out. Oh no, Ninette, I told myself, none of that, Ninette, or else it's the road to perdition. You have to prove you're worthy of that good conduct certificate, or else send it back to the director.

Everyone found my refusal reasonable. And right then, it blew through all of us like a breath of truth.

As for me, I never got the chance to go to school the way my son has. Grandma couldn't do without me around the house. She was so old she couldn't do her clients' laundry by herself anymore. People were starting to grumble about her work, and they threatened to cut us off if things continued like that.

So one day, Grandma says to me: little darling, it's time for you to get by on your own. Your little hands are still weak, but some day, they'll be strong enough to scrub and clean for the fancy ladies. You're twelve years old now. If you think I'm going to keep feeding a useless mouth, then you've got another think coming. Come on, get to work. You've got to help me, and be brave about it, and be extra careful and all.

What have you been doing up until today, anyway? You bring water from the fountain. Good. You get things for me from the grocer's. That's good, too. And you go to the baker's oven and the market. But the rest of the time? You dawdle around with "the ladies" like some kind of street dog. That's enough! One of these days, you're going to find me gone. Learn a trade, at least! You see how we're left to our own devices here. Not a penny do we get from charity. Only the whiners get that. We're too proud to beg, aren't we? We don't buy into that, do we? We've always relied on ourselves.

Ninette, Grandma continued that day, get a move on now, you hear? To begin with, sort this pile of laundry. Delicates to one side, the heavy stuff over here. And put the towels there, and the rags in this pile. Now, do a first soaking . . .

And the lesson continued like that, a little every day. And then, I learned how to iron. I picked up right away on how to iron pleats, gathers, and flounces. I took great pride when a client would say: bravo, Ninette. This looks like something that has come fresh from the Galeries Lafayette, it's so nice and crisp.

Then one day, who knows how, the wolf was on the prowl.

I don't have to tell you that he was good-looking and fun to be with.

That he had the sharp teeth and appetite of one looking for fresh meat. That much you've already figured out yourself. Where was he from? From the big city. What was he by trade? A mandolin player and a corpse washer for the Community.* Any work is better than none, right? You have to make a living however you can. And he knew how to laugh and drink and sing. He was good at cards and dice and dominoes, could cheat you out of a week's wages. He was a thief at heart, could come between you and your money without your even feeling it, painless, like a dentist, but better.

A rascal of his sort, there's no other like him in the world.

No sooner had he appeared on Sin Street than people were fighting over who would snatch him up for one of their parties, to sing the songs of Esmeralda the Algerian.

What Grandma said was this: he was a very close relative and we couldn't turn him away. But he took advantage of us, the rat, living off our hard work and getting drunk on our meager income.

It wasn't long after that Grandma passed away. That was worse for me than if someone had torn off one of my limbs.

But what good is it to reminisce and tell stories? It makes me want to ask the Almighty and his buddy the rabbi what they want from me, and what they've got against me and why they let so many bad people live in luxury and peace while the innocent have to pay and pay. How much? How long will this go on, this God's justice? And how come he, who can supposedly do all, has created scoundrels to harass poor folks and wolves to eat ignorant young girls? How come? I'd like him to answer me that one!

In everything that happened, how much was I responsible for? And my grandma, who was never honest enough to warn me of the danger? And what about the other guy, the wolf who abused me? And the whole society that owes me for everything it didn't do for me?

When I was by myself, I never despaired. Scrub and rinse, rinse and

---

* A "corpse washer" (*un laveur de morts*) refers to the practice of *tahara*, or purification of the dead according to Jewish law, and would be carried out by a member of the Hevra Kadisha (Jewish burial society). "The Community" refers to the Jewish community council, or *kahal*, which had the authority, among other things, to tax, issue legal rulings, and select community leadership.

scrub, sometimes a lot, sometimes a little, I always managed to eke out a living.

But the wolf clung to me like a vine, whispered sweet nothings in my ear and warmed my heart, took me to the pictures on Saturdays—with the money earned by the sweat of my brow, mind you, not his—and helped me forget my troubles. You'd have to be made of stone not to get attached to him.

"Ninette," he said to me one day out of nowhere, "it's not that you're stupid, but you're not crafty enough. If I were you, I'd go about things differently."

"I don't get it. Go about what things, and how, if you were me?"

"Don't play dumb, you know very well what I'm talking about. There you are, slaving away, working yourself to the bone day in day out, don't you ever get sick of it? How much have you managed to save? Where are your baubles and dresses, your fine linens and perfumes? With the work you do, you'll be old in four more years, if you haven't kicked the bucket by then. Leave it to me, I'll show you the way. If I didn't love you, baby, I would have dumped you a long time ago and beat it back to the capital. Now there's a city, my lovely, vast and beautiful, with movies and theaters, casinos and department stores, places to stroll downtown, places to visit outside town, beaches, too many good things to mention, all there for you to take in, to enjoy!

But here, ugh! You call this an avenue? Don't make me laugh! I could slip it into my pocket, it's so small. You have one movie theater to our ten, so many to choose from! And your municipal theater, seems like it's closed more often than it is open. There, we have a new production every week, oriental-themed gala events with entertainers like Habiba and Chamia and Bahia.* Dancing and singing, and exotic drinks with real fig *boukha* that goes down like milk.

---

* These were all Tunisian Jewish women musicians and/or dancers: Habiba Messika was Tunisia's most legendary star of the nineteen-twenties; "Chamia" refers either to Flifla Chamia or Ratiba Chamia; and "Bahia" is Bahia Chamia. In Tunisia, as across North Africa, Jewish women and men were disproportionately active in the music and entertainment industries.

Your cafés? Miserable compared to ours. With customers getting their shoes shined, and people spitting out in the open, all over the place. The sidewalks are disgusting.

And the flies and the mosquitoes and the dust and the sirocco. Doesn't that all start to add up? You turn around, and there's the train station. You take two steps and you're already at the other end of the town.

So, what do you say, do you really like it here so much? Listen to me, Ninette. I'll put it to you straight, I'm not going to waste my life away in this hellhole. I've made up my mind. Sell everything you have, and let's get out of here."

Did I really agree to follow him? I'm not sure I did. What was I thinking, then? How did it all happen, where and when? It's all a big *chakchouka** in my head. Sounds, images, a strange upside-down picture show! And lots of singing and spicy grilled meat and wine, oh lots of wine, treacherously sweet.

A strange hotel room. A bed. Get up, Ninette, I tell myself, something very bad is about to happen. Get up, Ninette, and get out of there. What's wrong, can't you put one foot in front of the other? You fool! Can it possibly be so hard to just get a move on? You're all fuzzy-headed, poor Ninette. You're listening to the phonograph. Yes, you like this song, don't you? Listen to it again. What does it remind you of? Your street, Sin Street. That street is in your blood, down to your marrow. When you were just a baby, you suckled vice like milk. Did you think you could escape it? Let him show you the way, like he says. Stop acting like this isn't you, old girl. The women in the neighborhood, your many godmothers, those who taught you to kiss, and without knowing it, to love perfumes, romances, alluring underwear, all those girls—Marietta, Lulu, Suzy, Carmen—all of them came to your initiation, your wedding.

---

* *Chakchouka* (sometimes transliterated as *shakshouka*), a staple of Tunisian cuisine, is a ragout made with eggs poached in a sauce of tomato, onion, garlic and cumin. The term itself means "mixture" in North African Arabic dialects. Used here metaphorically, it refers to a state of chaos or confusion.

Ninette, they called out, give us your hand and come join the circle. With us, Ninette, slave to males, pariah, garbage, rot. Come dance with us, Ninette, come join the dance.

No, I didn't understand right away what he had done to me. Except that my head was throbbing, and my legs and back felt sore. I could feel something hot and wet between my thighs.

Blood! My blood!

I screamed and fainted dead away.

You ask the name of this evil mandolin player, this corpse washer who does the devil's bidding?

For the name, I'll answer the way the rabbi taught me to: may his name and his memory be forgotten.

But who was he?

He was my uncle. And I was thirteen years old.

IV

Of course I've stopped coming to see you, Mr. Director, Sir. How could I show my face after what I told you last time? It's been six months since I told you the story of when and how I made my first stupid mistake (which the rabbi calls your first sin, Ninette). And you assure me you've forgotten everything. Well, I haven't. I turn them over and over, all day, all night, my bitter memories.

Whenever I start stirring up this muck, I make myself sick. Can't eat or sleep. But every so often, with one shrug of the shoulder, like I'm getting rid of some load I've been carrying, I just pack it all off to the devil. And I just go about my little business. It's just that this business of mine never seems to end. When will it all be over, when will the work all be done?

As for the boy, you say everything's going fine. Well, that's good news. I often say to myself: Ninette, your boy's in school. That's something to be happy about. In three or four years, he'll have a certificate. Then he'll learn a trade and become a man who will make his way in the world.

Come on, Ninette, that's something to be proud of, and the start of a new, better life for yourself, too.

I think about all this while these agile hands of mine move from one job to the next. I scour and polish my pots and pans with more heart. So much so that my new mistress—a Frenchwoman, quite the lady—says to me: oh, how she's changed, our Ninette! She's become so reasonable and hardworking! What's going on in that head of yours, Ninette? And yackety yack, like that, all praises and words that tickle your ear and warm your gut.

For the moment, I'm at peace. My mistress has no family except two dogs, a parakeet, and a canary. All things considered, it's a thousand times better than kids, don't you think, Sir?

Oh, and speaking of kids . . . no, between them and me, we just can't seem to get along. You're in a good position to know what I'm talking about. How do you feel about them? I've served some snot-nosed brats in my day, who look at you like you were nothing but a broom or something, and then they cry on purpose for no reason so that Madame will come and scold you!

When I think of everything I've had to endure, my blood starts to boil.

Why do I go that far? Well, since we're back to chatting now, let me tell you the rest of my story.

The rest of what story, you ask? Well, the rest of my life story, my novel, as they say.

. . . After what he went and did to me, my mandolin-playing uncle just up and dumped me. When I came to my senses and cried my eyes out, the hotel manager said to me: okay, sweetheart, time to clear out, hurry up now.

Since she didn't care a wit what had just happened to me, and didn't want the police to get mixed up in it, since back home, my disappearance had already been reported.

She took me to the train station, put a third-class ticket in my hand, and forward march, Ninette, back home to the bad old days.

I don't have to tell you that I wasn't a bit proud to be going home. Greeted like a dog with mange, I was, back on Sin Street. They were all whispering: there's a slut for you! Do you think she might be competition from now on? As if there wasn't enough cat-fighting going on around here. No, I think we're safe. Look at her, will you? Flat as an ironing board. And she wants to attract clients with that? She can't even wipe her own nose. What she needs is a good spanking, she does! And a hot chili right up the you-know-where. Then you'll see if she's still in the mood for messing around.

And I got the thrashing of a lifetime that I'll remember from here to kingdom come. Now that I think about it, I guess I understand what made them all so angry.

No matter how low you fall, you always have a little respect for something pure. A good girl who trots around in their midst, it's always a pleasant thing to behold, right? My protectors always hoped that I wouldn't turn out like them. And I went and betrayed their hopes. Ninette, the little laundress who took a wrong turn, was not the same Ninette as before. She wasn't worthy of friendship anymore. Since that's the way it is, go someplace else and start over, old girl, I thought.

I tried to imagine that this was just a thunderstorm over my head. Take shelter. Open an umbrella until it passes. They'll have to forgive you at some point, won't they?

Well, they never did. In the end, I got tired of it all.

I bundled up my things and went downtown to Rachela's—she's the woman from Djerba who runs a hotel-restaurant for Jews, Rue de la République. Ever heard of it?

Sure I have, Ninette. Rachela isn't a woman, she's a saint. All those whose lives are measured out in kilometers of highways and byways: professional beggars and occasional panhandlers, holy rabbis with an urge for travel, fake rabbis and charlatans in search of adventure; all the wanderers from the deep south that find their way up to the north and center of the country, all of them eventually end up at Rachela's.

Rachela is the Madonna of the flea-bitten masses, the wretched who have only pennies to spend for a meal and a bed next to another just like them who's already snoring away.

They pay conscientiously for the first few days. But after that . . . nothing! You can go to the courts or the police all you want, or to the devil for that matter, but you won't get anything out of those folks. Not even the whip to beat you with, Rachela, poor girl, or something that might cure you of that gullibility of yours.

When Rachela saw me, downcast and a bundle under my arm, she said:

Ah! Ninette, I know exactly what happened to you. Good thing your granny's passed away. She won't see you dishonored, poor kid. Come on in. This is the House of Lost Souls, as you well know. Don't worry, we'll find some crumbs for you to eat, too. As long as you've learned your lesson and you stick to the straight and narrow from now on. Because if you don't . . .

Nothing would have made me happier than to walk the line of virtue! But how, I ask you, when one of the hotel workers is chasing after you day and night?

He was a Jew from down south, a goofy sort who goes crazy at the sight of a skirt and can't keep his mind off you-know-what.

As soon as there's no one else around, he jumps on me, and I have to beat him off with my fists, and pinch him black and blue. One day, I almost poke his eye out. But he keeps coming back for more.

When nothing else worked, he changed tactics. He went for the heart, promised to marry me. Now that sounds more serious, I thought.

Truth be told, he wasn't such a bad fellow. If it hadn't been for the promise I'd made to Rachela, a thousand times I was on the verge of saying to him: no use losing sleep over a washerwoman like me. Go ahead, take what you want, since you seem so hell-bent on getting some, but don't forget I need my share too. What do you think, silly, that I don't feel the need just like you? A tender word here, a soft touch there, a couple of manly arms to hold you tight, that's what helps get you through your daily drudgery.

Once I'd gone down the list of all these whims and temptations, not surprising that I let myself be picked like ripe fruit. No need to yank too hard, one word and the apple fell right into his hand.

So that's all there is to love? Who'd have thought?

Biggest letdown in my life, I'd say. Talk about disillusions . . . That's what happens when you trust your imagination.

Once he'd satisfied his whim and his male pride, my onetime lover dumped me like the coward that he was, never imagining for an instant that I was still learning the lessons of life, and that I'd taken him seriously.

But nothing made me feel worse than the hurt I caused Rachela, who immediately figured out what had happened.

That look in her eyes, sometimes sad, sometimes angry, was the worst scolding I could have gotten from her.

You're a monster, Ninette, I said to myself. Betraying a wonderful woman like Rachela. You deserve a good beating, you do. And worse than that. Didn't you learn anything from your first experience? You still have illusions about men? Down on their knees and groveling at one moment, then once they've had what they were after, bye-bye sweetie, and who are you, never seen you before.

I bundled up my things again and got ready to leave. I planned to just slip away from the hotel. I just didn't have the heart to go say good-bye to Rachela and everyone. Not even to turn and have a last look.

But Rachela stopped me right on the threshold with one word: Ninette!

A long silence, then, in her soft voice: so, Ninette, you're on your way, are you? You're punishing yourself. That's good. It proves you still have a heart. So don't give up on yourself. You'll climb out of the horrible hole you've dug, don't worry. When and how? Well, I wonder sometimes. When I think of what might happen to you, it makes me shiver all over. Go on, now, and good luck to you. If you ever do get yourself in a bad fix, you know you can always come back to Rachela. For the moment, though, I can't keep you here, that's beyond even me.

She gave me a big hug and put a kerchief in my pocket with a little small change.

What kind of state I must have been in as I walked down the Rue de la République, I can't even imagine. The sun was so bright, and my prospects so dim!

The more I thought about it, the less certain I was of which way to go: return to Sin Street, or go stand in line at the unemployment office with the other hapless wretches looking for a way to earn their crust of bread?

I walked on without looking where I was going, when I suddenly felt that someone had taken my bundle.

It was Choua.

Come with me, he said in an authoritative voice. I could use your services.

Then, Rachela's words sprang to mind: you've dug yourself a hole, Ninette. And now you're going to jump right into it, and make things even worse for yourself, as if that were possible.

Once I heard the rabbi say in his Saturday sermon: you flee a serpent, and you land in the lion's mouth.

And that's just what happened to me.

Who was this Choua? Ah, Sir, let's not get ahead of ourselves. With your kind permission, I'll tell you all about him next time. Life is a long road still ahead. If I get everything off my chest at one go . . . , no, I can't do that. Otherwise, what pleasure would I have left in life, to keep on keeping on?

V

Yes, Mr. Director, Sir. It's Ninette again. Good day to you, first of all. And how have you been since the last time? And your family, and the kids? Isn't this job starting to get a little old for you now?

As for me, even though I'm not even thirty yet, I would love nothing better than retirement. I have to go to the Almighty and ask for it, I guess. Ninette is all washed up, nothing left of her. No more strength in my arms, no more solid calf muscles for all the running around I've had to do. The old carcass has gone through too much in the past. And what a past it was! There's a price for everything on this earth, the good and the bad. But especially the bad. That's something my son has to learn. You have to teach him that until it's etched deep into his brain.

One thing has been bothering me. When my little guy grows up, I'm worried he'll look down on his mother, about his birth and all, and the other adventures I've been through.

What I want is that he doesn't judge, but that he understands, so that he can forgive. What would someone else have done in my place? Given the constant harassment, she would have joined one of the local . . . establishments, of which there are plenty around here. Or she would have set herself up for business in some place like Sin Street.

But no, I always struggled to stay virtuous. If I fell, it's because someone tripped me.

My mortician? How old was I then, I ask you? And that gigolo at Rachela's hotel? That's what I get for trusting just any old suitor. I believed him, and why wouldn't I have? It's only natural. As for Choua . . . I was at my wits' end, out of a job and no place to live. I had to survive, first of all. Honor, virtue, that all has to wait when you're hungry.

You ask me who Choua was?

Listen, then, and I'll tell you.

In one of the most upstanding streets of the European part of the city, Choua had furnished himself a discreet apartment, where he came from time to time with other gentlemen to meet up with some lovely ladies, married or not, acquaintances or strangers. The story was that they would meet and have tea, and talk about the rain that was late this year and the sunny weather that made the farmers rage and enriched the usurers. You know, the usual stuff.

As the conversation grew more, shall we say, pleasant and interesting, one of the gents would take his lady friend to the little boudoir off the main room, where there were low sofas and mirrors everywhere so that you could see yourself from all sides, with all due respect to you, Sir.

What kind of music did they listen to in there—that, I was never to know. The rabbi taught me like this: they have eyes but don't see; ears but don't hear.

As for me, my role was to be deaf and blind. Otherwise, Choua, with his wandering hand . . .

But I can tell you everything, can't I?

Did I see dozens of gents parade through that apartment, or what? And women of all shapes, sizes and colors: mature and less so, dressed up, arrogant, shamefaced ones that hesitated at the door before diving in.

Little by little, I learned the story behind all those poor souls, those fools who came looking for what? Not the bare necessities, like my lady friends on Sin Street, but all the stuff that was just for show, like dresses and jewelry, caprices that their husbands couldn't afford.

None of the men were bachelors, either, but men married to nice ladies that I came to know.

The gents came there out of curiosity, mostly, in search of something new, or some special urge that they couldn't get their spouses to satisfy.

I sure felt bitter seeing this parade of characters whose secret I had to keep, and who couldn't pretend I didn't know.

One woman in particular, a young *Angliche,** in a bad marriage to an Italian, I believe. Fair-skinned, slender, and a pair of blue eyes, need I say more . . . ?

When they heard that if they were willing to pay, they could get her, she was the only one anyone wanted. Men of all sorts, stout and short, stout especially, freshly shaven and smelling of cologne, all short of breath at the idea of the choice little morsel they were about to consume.

Ah, Sir, society is rotten, isn't it? And from the top down, too. And to think that they're supposed to be the good folks. But I don't care. Nobody owes me anything.

But what was Ninette doing in this fine place, this shop of illusions, as folks called it? Well, she did just about everything. She waited on them in her lace smock and cap. She was the maid when it came to airing out

---

* A mispronunciation of "English," and a fusion of the French *"Anglais"* and "English," *Angliche* could refer to an indigenous young woman whose family had acquired British protection, or to an émigrée from the United Kingdom. This "English girl" is depicted as exotic in this southern Mediterranean milieu.

the bedding, straightening up, cleaning the toilets, putting away the liquor bottles and mopping the floor.

And I was also a substitute. In addition to everything else! Yes, and my turn came around more often than it should have.

For instance, if a lady guest expected at four o'clock for tea doesn't show? Choua bolts into the kitchen and goes: Ninette, put on some makeup and slip into what's-her-name's negligee, or Miss So-and-So's lounging gown and get yourself into the living room, quick! You get it? Put on the smile, act the lady, give them a show, right?

The trick worked most of the time, and I managed to pick up quite a few gifts meant for someone else, in addition to hugs and kisses.

I was allowed to keep those, but—you guessed it—Choua took back the gifts, whether or not I was ready to part with them.

How much was I paid for all my work? Not a thing! I was fed and housed, wasn't that enough? Choua said I should be as grateful to him as a faithful dog, since he was the one who saved me by getting me off the street. Without him, I would have been lost, plunged forever into misery.

Well, I wasn't going to stand for that, no Sir. Who did he think he was, anyway? Just so that his clients wouldn't leave unsatisfied when a woman didn't show, I had to replace her? Does he call that saving me or digging me in deeper?

Who do you think you're kidding, my old Choua? You're as big a scoundrel as the others, exploiting the misery and weakness of a woman. That's your kind of morality.

And the days went by, each one as gloomy as the one before, without a glimmer of hope for me to get out.

Poor Ninette, I said to myself. This time you've really touched bottom. Your mandolin-playing uncle forced himself on you. You were too young, you couldn't have understood. You can be forgiven for that time. Your guy at the hotel? He got you in the end, but only after you fought him off for months. You gave in to him, because you thought you felt something for him. Say what you want, but you can't deny you had a little crush on him, can you? So on that score, you're also forgiven, since there was some feeling in the mix. But now? Try to answer for this one, if you dare! Now that you're bedding down with any old bourgeois who shows up, and that you don't know from Adam, what do you have to say about that, Ninette?

Go on, old girl, go throw yourself into the sea rather than continue this dog's life you're leading.

And I kept thinking: are you that stupid that you let yourself be shut up in this prison? For what crime? If you had done something stupid, I'd say: fine, Ninette, stay where you are and die there, you deserve it. But all you're guilty of is trust. Run away, then! Go on, run away! Find a way to toss your fine protector overboard and go breathe some new air.

Once I'd plotted my escape, I announced to Choua one day, like this:

Choua, I said, you're a good guy, and all that. You picked me up off the street and provided me room and board. Thank you. But it's not enough to eat and sleep and receive clients. It's no better than Sin Street, in fact, if you don't mind my saying so. I haven't seen the sky in so long, I forget what color it is. I'm suffocating in this box. I want to see my friends, my family, go visit them, find out what's happening in their lives. Have there been deaths, births, engagements, weddings? Who, when, how, where? I want to know these things! Silliness? You might say that, but for us women—the rabbi says our heads are full of air—these are the most important matters to us.

And Choua let me leave!

No, Ninette, if you go back to that house of perdition, it'll have to be feetfirst in a wooden box.

And I ran to the rabbi, not the one from Djerba with the long beard and the pretty sermons about the Messiah and other lies and deception. No, but to the Grand Rabbi with the little gray eyes and who wears a turban that came straight from Jerusalem.

"Good day, Rabbi," I said as I entered his study room, all humble and small.

"Peace be upon you, my daughter. What is it you have come for?"

"Rabbi, I've come to ask you a favor."

"And how can I help you. My powers are weak, but God is great."

"That's just what I was thinking. Only the rabbi could get me out of this fix . . . you see, I'm an orphan, no father or mother."

"What's your family name?"

"Chouchan."

"Chouchan? I don't know that name. But that doesn't matter."

"It doesn't, does it? Chouchan, Sadik, Berrebi or Azria, we are all children of God, right?

"That is right, my daughter."

"I'm an orphan, as I said. Until now, I've been a laundress in a bad place. Excuse me, Rabbi, I don't dare say it any other way. And now that I'm all grown up, I'm afraid that if I continue to have bad examples all around me, something bad might happen. Can you save me, find me a place with a good family? You'll see how dedicated I can be."

"You are right, my daughter. I'll see what I can do for you."

"Rabbi, it's very urgent. I can't return to the place I came from. I'm in the street, completely on my own."

"How do you expect me to find you a place just like that, in five minutes? Are you mad, girl?

"I know it's hard, but what can I do?"

"This isn't like going to the market and finding what you want right away, the same as every day."

"If you can't find me a place by tonight, I'm lost. And God alone knows whose sin it will be."

"You're certainly persistent! All right, stay here in the meantime. You are a daughter of my race, I cannot abandon you in your hour of need."

He straightened his turban, took his cane and coughed several times, as if to hearten himself. At the door, he turned around and asked:

"I hope that you are serious about all this."

"Of course I am."

"And that you don't steal things, at least . . . "

"Oh, Rabbi, don't you see I have an honest face?"

". . . and you don't lie?"

"Rabbi, how can you say that?"

"Because I'm going to recommend you to a very distinguished family. A widow with a son, no one else. They are foreigners who have just arrived. With a little luck, I'll get you a place as servant with these good people who were recommended to me by a colleague. Stay here for a half hour or so, and I'll be right back."

And he came right back, the good rabbi, with good news about the job and wonderful conditions!

Ah! Why didn't I break my leg on the way to the rabbi's! Then none of what was to about to happen would have taken place . . .

I can't blame the rabbi, it wasn't his fault at all, the poor man. But he was misled. You think people are good and upstanding, and then at the least little thing, the mask falls and you see the real face, the one they were so good at hiding.

They're distinguished people, the rabbi had told me. Well, me, I would say they were a couple of brutes.

Well, Sir, it's about time I was on my way. Why am I leaving, you ask?

So you want me to let out everything I know at one go, everything that has been weighing on my heart, heavier than the stone they'll lay on me in my grave when I'm gone?

Oh, no Sir, not for today. I've been chatting away for a while now. I have to get back and take in my laundry from the terrace after this nice sunny day we've had, the kind of sun that warms you to the bone. Ninette doesn't have servants at home, she isn't rich enough for such things. That will come some day, I'm not saying it won't. But not for now.

So, I'll be off now; I'll have to come back on a day that's as dark and gloomy as my life story. Then the heart harmonizes with the weather, and I'll be able to open up the dam and let the stories flow, and you'll hear stories. Oh, the stories you'll hear!

VI

Of course I'm not hiding, Mr. Director, Sir. Why would I be trying to avoid you?

Six months since you last saw me, really? How time flies, doesn't it? Could that be? Me, I always think I'll never make it to the end.

The boy is doing well, though. Every month, he brings me a list of his grades, as long as my tab at the grocer's, and he says: have a look, Mama, see how well I'm doing in school.

So I lean down and pretend to read what's scribbled on the paper in front of me. And we burst out laughing, the two of us. But I go ahead and sign anyway, pressing my ink-stained thumb to the paper with all my might.

You must have had a good laugh, too, seeing my thumbprint!

Laugh all you want now, but I swear I'll get some education later on, when I have some free time.

Dreams, you say? Yes, but beautiful dreams, like all crazy people have. I'll have my son teach me . . . since by then, he'll have a good job, good connections, a lovely wife, I don't want him to be ashamed of an ignorant mother.

But for now, unfortunately, I'm working myself into the ground. How am I supposed to learn when I can't remember a darn thing? My head is like a sieve. Put something in it today and it'll be gone tomorrow.

I forget everything. Only thing I remember are my misadventures, my past pain, and that's because it's all written right onto my body. All it takes is a word, a gesture, a song, and click, like a light switch, the memories kick in and I see a parade of people from the past, and all the misery and shame they bring along.

It's Choua and his house of ill repute; it's the little Jew from the south; it's the mortician with his mandolin. They cast a shadow on my life that blinds me to everything else.

But the other one, the father of my boy, the man who got what he wanted out of me so many times, and then dumped me when I got pregnant, I hate him worst of all, so much that I don't remember who he is. You could point to him in a crowd, and I'd say I don't know him! My mind refused to retain his features.

All of that by way of introduction to the next installment of my story, when the rabbi gave me that bit of paper with a recommendation to those new arrivals. I was so proud of myself: bravo Ninette, I said, for having such a good idea this time around. No one can deny that, can they?

The mother and her son only, the rabbi had said, and not only that, but a very distinguished pair, it seemed. Now that's some good luck, I'd say. And you thought you were lost forever, and jinxed for eternity. Always griping and never satisfied, weren't you? Now that's a flaw we'll have to fix, won't we?

But here's the thing that was troubling me. What does that mean exactly, "distinguished people"? Maybe they don't walk or talk or eat like everyone else on Jerusalem Street, Sinai Street, or Sin Street . . .

You're awfully curious, Ninette, aren't you? And impatient, too. Just wait and see, and then you'll talk.

So, we arrive at the address indicated, me, the letter and my little bundle of belongings.

It was the mother who opened the door. A Jewess, like other Jewesses I've known, plump, chubby-cheeked, potbellied, but with a stern air about her, the high-and-mighty type that shuts your trap just looking at her. Old? Not exactly, but well past forty, if you get my meaning.

She gave me the once-over, so brash I almost opened my mouth to let her look inside while she was at it. Have a look at my teeth, ma'am, all present and still in good shape.

She clapped, and called for her son to enter the room.

"This is our new maid. It seems she's a fine laundress, so that should make you happy. You'll finally have well-ironed shirts."

"For that, boss, you can rest assured, it's my specialty."

"Please Mademoiselle, call me Madame."

"Sorry, from now on I'll call you Madame, but as for me, I'm Ninette, not Mademoiselle."

The young man, long-legged, a little over twenty, was the spitting image of the mother, but more graceful. The resemblance between them was striking. The look in the eyes, especially, something fleeting. The son wasn't as self-assured as his mother, but instead seemed mild-mannered, hesitant and shy, or just plain stupid. Or all of that together. From the way he would say yes mother and no mother, I figured out that she kept him on a leash, and that he was still clinging to her skirts in a way.

So I thought: with the son, it should be manageable. We'll find a way to make like friends. As for the mother, with her snobby airs, she's got me scared. We'll have to see.

All right, Ninette, I say to myself, you didn't come here to be criticizing folks and finding fault. Do your job, and don't give a hoot about the rest. How about your own character, after all? You've been known to run off at the mouth, haven't you? You're going to have to learn to hold your tongue, to be all yes-ma'am-no-ma'am and polite. If you can't get along with these folks, I don't know what's going to become of you, poor girl.

That's how I turned over the situation in my mind.

No use lying about it, I was paid regularly and well fed and nicely housed in a little furnished room up on the terrace.

But these folks wanted their money's worth.

So, no more going out, no more strolls around the city. Cooking, washing, ironing. An endless cycle that had me doing all three at once sometimes.

At first, it was a nice change from Choua's house of ill repute, and I dazzled their highnesses with my know-how and energy.

As for them, they were out most of the day. Judging from the bits and pieces of conversation I overheard, they spent their day running from their lawyer's office to the bailiff's office, and from the bailiff's to the judge's chambers.

Some Bedouins owed them money, lots of money. So they were running around trying to find a way to get something back, even in grain or olives.

Often, they'd be gone all morning, then come home for a quick lunch, and then leave again in their car along with the bailiff to go impound some miserable piece of property.

That's how they spent the winter. Toward the end of the season, the son got fed up with these errands all over the *bled*.* He was tired of being dragged around by his mother who, I have to say, did boss him around like a drill sergeant or something. They quarreled over it.

So eventually, the mother continued going out every day, but alone now, while the son stayed behind, wandering from room to room, not knowing what to do with himself.

If you were a miserable Jew like all the others, and had to earn a living, I said to him in my head, you'd see that you wouldn't have time to be bored. But here you are, twiddling your thumbs while everyone else is slaving.

I even think that, when it came to education, he wasn't exactly a heavyweight. Otherwise, he would have bought newspapers or books to find out what was happening in the rest of the world.

In a word, he was a perfect loafer. And when you have nothing to do, you're bored. And when you're bored, you start looking around for entertainment. How? Well, you'd talk to the wall if it came to that, but even better, with Ninette, who isn't the dumbest person around, and who has a nice little stock of direct experience with people and life in general.

Better believe I interested him! He even grabbed a chair and sat right down in front of me while I was sewing or ironing or peeling potatoes, and asked me all kinds of questions: and your mother, Ninette, what did she do? And your grandmother, what did she do, too? And your little nephews and second cousins once removed, what did they do? Before coming here, what did you used to do? Where did you sleep, and what did you eat?

In short, he wanted to know everything there was to know about me. Of course, I told him only what I could reasonably tell him, right? I arranged my story so as to dodge the whole Choua issue.

To hear me tell it, you'd think Ninette was still pure as the driven

---

* *bled*: a North African Arabic term derived from *bilad* or *balad* [country]. *Bled* takes on multiple meanings in Maghrebi Arabic [Darija], in which it may be used to indicate country, land, or homeland. Depending on context, *bled* can refer to a town, city, or village, but also to the countryside or rural areas. The term has been appropriated into modern colloquial French.

snow, and didn't know anything about anything concerning wolves and the little girls that fall into their clutches.

I meant no harm by it all, nothing up my sleeve, as they say. I enjoyed having someone to talk to. You can get pretty bitter from always looking inside yourself, going over and over the same stories in silence, right? So I did everything I could to be entertaining and keep the boss's attention, since he was simpleminded enough to find me interesting.

One thing led to another, and pretty soon, we had gotten close. Behind the mother's back, you ask? Oh, no! She was smart enough to pick up on it right away. And dishonest enough to try and make the most of the situation in favor of her son, which is to say, in her own favor, too. But I didn't realize that until much later.

You see, I was so concerned about keeping up my innocent appearance, about just staying nice and friendly with the guy, I never suspected that the whole thing was a trap.

Life's funny sometimes, isn't it? Three of us in the house, living together, our lives stitched together, side by side. We thought we knew each other, thought we could read the other person's eyes, like through a crystal-clear window. And yet! Each of us had something in the back of our minds, it turned out.

The mother, who must have been quite the beauty back in her youth, was saying to herself (and she was even nasty enough to admit to it, the day of our big fight!): we know how things work. A young man needs a woman. You need that as much as food on the table and your forty winks, right? My son here is growing up. Our situation is still too messy right now for me to be thinking about getting him married. So, instead of having him go to the brothels and get some awful disease, why not let him pick the most available flower? Maids are supposed to do everything, service with a smile and all, even serve as mistress.

So that's how this tender mother reasoned!

And what were the son's thoughts on the matter?

Don't go looking at me now, flat and bony as I am. Back then, I was still fresh and pretty and desirable.

The son, who definitely had his eye on me, thought I wasn't so bad for a little fling, despite our class difference. So what did he want? He was torn between daring to take the first step and fearing I'd send him packing. His hesitation had something to do with the friendship that had grown between us. We'd been playing a brother-and-sister game up till then, and it seemed strange to suddenly find that impure impulses were burning in your veins.

And what was going on in my little head, and in my heart, all this time? I had no idea, really. His awkwardness, his shyness, that hangdog look in his eyes, all that made me uneasy. I was unhappy at the idea that I was about to give in. I was even unhappier at the thought that, no matter what I did, the end result would be the same: I was going to get sacked.

It must have happened one day when we had both reached a boiling point, knowing what was going to happen. A little song was singing inside each of us, a little silent duet, just like at the movies, a song about kisses and seventh heaven and everlasting love and flowers that open at the touch of butterflies.

And a bunch of romantic junk like that.

But who was the first to start, who gave the other a look, a hand, then lips, then went all the way?

No one's to blame, really. We both wanted it. But once we started, the devil only knew how and where we were going to stop.

At night, when all was quiet in the house, in the street, in the neighborhood, he would sneak up to my room on the terrace like a thief. He would scratch at the door, call my name through the keyhole, and in a distressed voice say: Ninette, open up!

So there I was, unable to breathe, and I waited a bit before sliding the bolt over, gripped suddenly by fear and remorse.

Once, twice at most, nothing wrong with that, right? But every night, no! He was going to get me in the family way at this rate, the idiot, and then what would become of me?

But for once he was smart enough to read my mind. He swore that if this were to happen, he'd marry me for sure.

Ah, the eternal promise that men make and women pretend to believe, all the while knowing it's a load of baloney. Just the excuse they're waiting for to force the issue and get some attention.

I don't think I ever really fell for it completely. But it had been more than a year since I'd been with a man. I had some reserves to spend, in other words. Fear, modesty, restraint—come on now, I just tossed all that to the wind and threw myself body and soul into the swirl of love.

And what about the mother? Oh, she knew exactly what was going on, and even became our accomplice. It was obvious from the way she switched from being so distant and reserved to giving me little gifts, like a tube of lipstick or a little bottle of lavender essence.

I've always had a weakness for perfumes. They really make me lose hold of my senses, feel drunker than on alcohol. And the mother knew that, the shrew.

Well, you know what they say about going to the well too often. But this time, the bucket didn't come up empty, but overflowing!

When I realized I was in trouble, as they say, I thought: okay, Ninette, don't be a ninny, wake up! You're usually more resourceful than this. You know where babies come from, and it's not from storks. You know all about how they're made, in fact. What were you thinking?! When a man sticks his filthy stuff up there, what do you expect? Of course the seed gets planted and the fruit grows.

Things were getting serious. I counted the days, but that welcome flow didn't come to my rescue. Another month began. Ten, twenty, twenty-five, thirty, and now sixty days since my last time. Sixty! I repeated the number mechanically. I saw it dancing before my eyes, on the furniture I dusted, on the pots and pans I scoured.

Let's count it out again, I said to myself, in the vain hope that I might have miscalculated. So when was the last time you went to the *mikvah*?*

---

* The French text simply says, "bain rituel," or ritual bath, but *mikvah* is more commonly used in English.

Such and such a day. Okay, then this happened, then that happened. Fine, now add it up.

There could be no doubt. Pregnant, and soon into the third month. Well, you're a piece of work, you are, poor Ninette! Congratulations on a job well done, letting someone do that to you. This time you've really been had, but good! You thought you could fool with Mother Nature, but she's stronger than all of us. The seed took, and the fruit is on its way. This dizziness you've been feeling, the nausea, loss of appetite, hot flashes. That's nothing, all that. Put your thinking cap on and come up with a way out of this!

I began by locking the boss out of my room. Then, after rushing through my afternoon work, I ran around from one back-alley* doctor to the next to find a way to unload my burden.

If there's a hell where you have to make a little stopover to chat with Satan in person on your way up to heaven, then I'll have a dispensation, I'll go straight up, express train, because in this dog's life I've led, I've already been to hell and back.

Who can top me when it comes to swallowing bitter pills, drinking disgusting home brews, hearing about old wives and their remedies?

But no, that kid had taken root and was there to stay. It was like a nail in concrete. You'd have had to bring down the whole wall to get it out. For me, too, you'd have had to take a butcher's knife and cut me open, right here, way deep, from top to bottom, to get to that little rascal that was hardly anything at all at that point, and who would cause me such trouble later on.

Once I finally realized there was no way out, I grabbed the mama's boy and got straight to the point with him:

"In a few months, I'm going to be a mother. And it's yours. What are you going to do about it?"

He went all pale at first, tried to laugh to keep up appearances and all, but then started thinking about what I had said.

---

* The original French uses the word "matrone," a term that formerly referred to a woman who practiced midwifery and abortion.

Good God, he had the dumbest expression on his face! To think I
had given myself to a dimwit like him. I had a good mind to grab him by
the shoulders and kick him out of the house for good. No, this was not a
man but a mollusk, a slug, with no will of his own, no substance. That's
what I had standing in front of me.

He walked away without the slightest promise, not a word of consolation or regret for the fine mess he'd gotten me into.

In short, I'll spare you the details of the scene where I dragged the
mother and son before the Grand Rabbi!

The mother brought damning testimony against me: the version according to Choua, who had never forgiven me for running out on him.

And Choua, the miserable wretch, said whatever he wanted, trotted
out the story of the mortician and the suitor at Rachela's hotel, laid out
in stark detail everything from my past, all that weight I'm still carrying
to this day, but that I wasn't responsible for.

Because of Choua, I wasn't able to prove that it was the son of this
foreigner who'd gotten me pregnant.

The rest, Sir? You want to know how I managed after all that?

The Grand Rabbi got me six months' wages plus compensation for
the delivery. Go, my daughter, he said in the end, and Godspeed!

After the rabbi had given his verdict, the others just fled the scene,
like a couple of criminals. I ran to catch up with them. When I finally
did, I took off a shoe, and there in front of everyone on Rue Pasteur—
hairdressers, grocers, and short-order cooks—I gave the mother a thrashing she's not likely to forget anytime soon.

As for the son, I spit in his face. He bolted from the scene, looking
like a wet hen, without daring to even look back.

And me? I was on the verge of a breakdown. And in front of all the
onlookers, I collapsed onto the steps of one of the shops and burst into
tears, and cried my eyes out.

Come now, Ninette, after all, you are the granddaughter of the granddaughter of the wandering Jew. Put your bundle back on your shoulder
and head out to meet your fate, whatever it may be. Rue de la République,

on the doorstep of the Hotel for the Weary, Rachela watched me approach with those sweet eyes of hers, awaiting the return of the little lamb who'd gone astray.

VII

Mr. Director, Sir, this time you're going to rejoice along with me. For once, I'm bringing you some good news.

Seems a new *caïd** has just been appointed to our good city. Oh no, he's no ignoramus. He studied French and all to become a lawyer. How about that? You know how lawyers are, such good talkers—it's their job, no one holds it against them—that they can turn black into white and make an assassin innocent, right there in the hands of the police.

The *caïd* says he's going to find a way to get a birth certificate for my son. Even without a known father? You got it! Even without a known father. I told you that lawyers could do anything, didn't I?

And how is it that Ninette has connections in high places now, eh? She goes to chat with the *caïd* just as if he was Zegnini the grocer or Tektouk the baker.

So let me tell you the story behind it all.

Mr. Joseph, the sheikh for all us native Jews here, he met up with me recently. And he says: so, is it true, Ninette, that you have a kid that's not registered? How come?

And I told him a short version of the story of my life, since he wasn't yet sheikh when all that stuff I told you was happening to me.

Mr. Joseph, moved by my plight, says: well, I'll be! That's some story you've got there. You can count on me, Ninette. The *caïd* is a man of law who knows how things work. Rest assured, we'll do what it takes.

Too bad for me that Mr. Joseph wasn't sheikh back when all this was happening. Things would have turned out very differently.

And what would have become of me without Rachela? I would have

---

* Arabic for "leader," the word *caïd* [ka'id] refers to a local official or governor selected from among the indigenous population under French colonial rule. The term went on to acquire the meaning, in metropolitan France, of "top dog" or "bigwig," especially (but not exclusively) of the criminal underworld.

had my baby in some alley, like a dog. And she had too much else to do to be running to the *caïd*'s office to explain what all was going on with me.

So let me pick up where I left off. You remember that I beat the mother and spit at the son. You can only imagine that after all that, I didn't have an ounce of strength left. But I grabbed my bundle, and with the other little bundle I was carrying inside me, I reached Rachela's hotel dead tired. That good woman took my things and gave me her arm to help me up the stairs.

Oh, you poor child! What in the world have you done now?

That was the only word of reproach I ever heard from her. She then took me to a little room with a bed and said: this will be your room until you deliver. We'll see what happens after that.

Troubled, sick, and disgusted with everything, I didn't do much around the hotel. But Rachela left me free to do what I wanted. There were days when I didn't even get out of bed, exhausted after a sleepless night. It became a habit of mine to lie wide-awake, staring at the ceiling.

Toward morning, I'd doze off a bit, but the little fellow I was carrying would start kicking me in the ribs to wake me up.

Oh, did it ever hurt! He would squirm around and get comfortable, the little bastard! He was already bruising me, I could feel something hard sitting there, almost at my heart, and a big ball weighing on me down below that must have been the head.

And I would just cry and cry. From now on, he would be a part of my life, this stranger's seed, maybe a bad seed. Would he turn out like his father, a coward, a spineless fool? I already hated him.

Rachela soothed me: my dear, you never know when or where luck might come your way. Who says you're not carrying the Messiah? Every Jewess lives in that hope, you know. But nothing can get accomplished without pain. Let's have a look at you. Hmm, it feels like you're just about ready, ripe as a date. It'll be any day now, I'd say. You'll need patience, though. You have to bring him into the world in joy. He didn't ask to come, after all. You have no right to snub him. Heavens no! The more you complain, the worse your misfortune will seem. So why don't you get out of bed and go get some fresh air. It'll do you good. Don't be ashamed to strut that belly of yours. Good-hearted people know who the guilty party is in all this. Just because you come from common folk doesn't mean you've less right to be forgiven than some little upper-class twit who gets herself knocked up by her boyfriend or fiancé.

She was trying to talk sense to me, but I was deaf to it all, and stayed in bed, weary of life and wishing I could just die, and put an end to my troubles, my shame, and the baby along with them.

I thought to myself: if I could die, that would be two fewer miserable people in the world. What's in store for the two of us, me an unwed mother, and the kid an outlaw, a fatherless wretch, a bastard, if you don't mind my calling things by their name?

And the gloomy days went by, and the sleepless nights piled up.

And then, my memory went blank.

Later on, Rachela told me how it all happened: early one morning, around dawn, she heard little mewing sounds followed by groans. Then a moment of silence. Then cries, mewing, and groans started up again. Several times, she sat up in bed, thinking she was having a nightmare of some sort. Drowsy and a little fearful, she stayed in bed instead of going to find out where the sound was coming from. But when the mewing noises became insistent, she figured it out and headed straight for my room.

She found me lying on my back, and between my bloodstained thighs was a little wailing being.

"Ninette, have you lost your mind? Are you trying to do yourself in or what? Why didn't you call for me? Having a baby all by yourself, that's just craziness! Let's see what you've had, at least. A boy! Be glad, you've just given birth to the person who will save you some day. We'll love the little thing together, won't we now?"

Rachela woke up everyone in the hotel, sent for a midwife, changed my sheets, and gave me my baby to hold close.

That little reddish, puckered-up thing, my future savior? You've got to be kidding. He's ugly as sin!

The next day, and the following days, until the eighth, the whole city's worth of curious gossipers dropped by to congratulate me, not without a hint of sarcasm.

Face against the wall, all I could do was cry. If I had been able to speak, and answer back to each and every one with a little tidbit I happened to know about their own personal history—not always a pretty picture—that would have set the cat among the pigeons, wouldn't it have?

On the eighth day, the day of circumcision, some real drama took place in the hotel courtyard.

The father is supposed to be the one who holds the baby while the knife-wielder cuts the bit of skin. But where was the father? Doesn't matter, we'll find some man of goodwill. But what should the baby be named? Ask Ninette. But Ninette is still in her deaf-mute state. No, she doesn't want this child. We should just turn it over to the auctioneer to sell, or give it away to a childless couple.

Finally, they came to an agreement as to what to name the baby. Look, since he's a little Jew, we'll call him Israel.

It was simple as pie, and all these arguments and all that shoving and jousting could have been avoided, which would have made Ninette happy, since she was at the end of her tether.

So let's get this thing over with, the prayers and ceremony, and hurry up and leave the hotel in peace, and Ninette to her misery.

A little while later, I held my baby up in front of me, and then, as if I was dealing with a reasonable person capable of understanding me, I said to him:

"So, it's just the two of us now, little stranger's seed. You wanted to come into the world, did you? Well, here you are, and a good job you did of it, too, son of mine!

You must be one stubborn little critter, with will to spare, because even though I tried just about everything, I wasn't able to wash you out of me.

You have come, no doubt about that. But let me tell you, it's no fun. Life is beautiful for the tough ones, the clever ones, those who know how to get around. There aren't many of those, you know. Those are the ones in charge, who order everyone else around. And the rest of us, there are thousands who are fighting over a job or a crust of bread. The dumbest, the fools, the flock of sheep. They get led around however and wherever the top dogs say. And what about you, now? Which side will you be on? How will you act toward me? Cowardly, like your mandolin-playing great-uncle, or stupidly, like your idiot father, or maybe you'll end up a pimp like Choua? What do you say? Oh, why in God's name did you want to come into this world? Just to add to my already unbearable burden? What are you doing here, since there's no place for either of us in this world? What name am I going to use to introduce you? Me and you, we'll be held at arm's length, like something contagious. You shouldn't have done it, son of mine. It's not good, what you've gone and done! You should have left me alone to wander down this damn road I'm on. Maybe I might have actually gotten somewhere, in the end. But there are two of us now, and with your appetite for life, you'll take everything I've got, my days, my nights, my time off, my wages.

That's why I hate you. I don't even have any milk to give you. See for yourself if my breasts aren't flat, emptied by pain and sorrow. So what will you eat? I have no idea. And you scream and fuss and keep the whole house awake.

That's right, sharpen that tongue of yours now. You'll be needing it later when the time comes to grumble. The louder you holler, the better you'll be heard, and respected, too. Your mother didn't make a big enough pest of herself. For instance, she could have pulled on the beard of the rabbi who credited Choua's lies and falsehoods. She could have slapped your miserable father silly. Maybe they would have concluded that she was right, if only to get her to stop kicking up such a fuss.

Right, fine, we sit here and chat like there's no tomorrow, and you just keep on bawling. Quiet now, little man. Everyone's going to wake up, and what am I supposed to tell them? That you don't want to nurse, and that I'd like to be rid of you? That you're a bother and an annoyance! That you weigh heavy in my arms, and that I carry you around like a big ball of guilt!

I'll say all of that, I swear!

You cry like a wimpy little girl, and for what? What'll happen later, when everyone turns against you, when you have real troubles of your own? You'll have to learn, like your mother did, how to live with hunger and humiliation. Hunger especially.

If your father had any guts, he would have felt something at the news of your birth. He would have come to us. But no! He abandoned you. What's keeping me from doing the same?

Who are you to me, anyway? I don't know you from Adam. And now you're here, demanding things, not leaving me a moment's peace. Well, who's going to satisfy my needs, tell me? I'm crying just like you, and just as revolted. But my tears are all inside, and all those bitter words just get stuck in my gullet."

I went on letting off steam like that for quite some time. Then, I noticed that the little one had calmed down, almost as if he understood what I'd said. He looked at me with those big eyes for just a second, then he turned his head and looked to the light that was streaming in through the window. It was a bright red winter sun that was just rising. I shuddered with cold at the sight of the damp walls across the way, and the steamed-up windows.

I started up again, this time talking more to myself than to him: "Son, don't get too comfortable now. For the moment, we're sheltered from the worst, but what's to become of us tomorrow? Where are we going to lay down our load? Tell me that, little pumpkin. Looking a little tired, you are. Something hurting you somewhere? And you're hungry and thirsty, too, I'll bet. Tough luck for you that you were born of me, Ninette. When you walk down the street, folks will point and laugh. And you'll be cursing your mother's womb, and the hour when you were conceived. You see? A moment's folly means a lifetime of suffering. And suffer you will, my little one! And here I am, already mistreating you myself! As if it was me that was your enemy! Is God punishing me twice over? After giving me a son with no father, he's hardening my heart, too?

Come over here, let me have a look at you.

You're really not that bad, despite your wrinkly face. You're good-looking, in fact. Why didn't I see that before? The way you look at me, boldly, so confident, I'm starting to feel like I already love you.

Hey, don't take too seriously what I was saying a little bit ago. Bad memories started coming back, memories of bygone days.

Whatever I might say or do, you're mine and I can't—I won't—ever abandon you.

What? Let go of you, deliver you into the hands of strangers? Lies and deception! Come here into my arms, little love. Put your mouth to my miserable breast and see what you can get. You can take my blood if you need it!

From now on, there will be no one but you, I swear to it. And now that we've made up and all, we'll move ahead in life, struggle along, a couple of loners, until the sun shines a little warmer on us poor rejects."

VIII

So, it's to say farewell and all that I've come by today, Mr. Director, Sir.

We're leaving your school. Well, not me; my son, I mean. But me too, I've known you for six years now, and I guess I consider myself one of your pupils, in a way. Oh, not the smartest of them, that's for certain; the dumbest, I'd say, the last in the class, but I'd say I've earned an A+ for effort and the will to do well.

My son is leaving for a vocational school now. Thanks to you, once again, he was admitted even without all the right papers.

The rabbi often says that that which has been bent cannot be made straight again. I don't believe that one bit. Just this once, though, I think he might be right. You see, neither the *caïd*, nor the sheikh, nor you were able to find a way of getting my son registered on the books. Let's face it, you can't create a father out of thin air for a child who's almost twelve years old.

Twelve years old! It's been a long road, hasn't it?

To think I've lived that whole time all alone with my son! That we've managed to get this far unharmed, that's a miracle in itself!

Of course, I knew that our stay at Rachela's was only going to be temporary.

Just six months after my giving birth, poor Rachela was facing ruin, and was so discouraged that she sold her place for a song and went back to Djerba to live with her sister.

You can only imagine what our good-bye was like. Twenty times we bade each other farewell, and twenty times we flew back for a last hug, crying like babies.

With my bundle of rags in one arm and my son in the other, I headed straight back to Sin Street, the way a lost animal returns to the fold.

Lucky for me, my old room happened to be empty, the one with the little patio where I used to hang out the washing for the "ladies."

I whitewashed the walls, bought some cheap pottery for the kitchen, a washbasin, some soap and salts, and set up shop once again as a washerwoman.

And to make it perfectly clear that I'd broken off with men for good, I went down to see Panayotti, the Greek, the local wine merchant. With a paintbrush and a piece of board I'd brought along, I had him write, in magnificent letters:

No Yousse Nocking Heer.
This Is A Kleen Howsse*

This is the sign I nailed to the outside wall. Then, with the door locked and my baby in my arms, I headed out to visit the little shops and stands to drum up some laundry business.

It had been three years since I'd left Sin Street to go down to the city.

You can imagine how much things had changed. It was cleaner than before, but drearier at the same time. No more singing, no more bursts of laughter!

Just like your heart, Ninette, I said to myself. Then, on second

---

* The French reads: "Inutil frappe à cet porte. Cet une meson onnette." The English "translation" makes similar phonetic transcriptions and errors. Danon's note in the original indicates that this is an authentic sign that could be seen all over the red-light district of Sfax at that time.

thought, when all the lights went on after dark, when the warm night air was filled with the aroma of grilled meat, hot bread, incense and cologne, and the sound of the Arab women's *cab-cab*,* I felt differently: no, Ninette, you're seeing everything through the eyes of your soul.

It's the same filth and the same degradation as during your grandma's time. Only you're all upset at finding yourself back at square one. You thought you'd made it out of Sin Street for good. You left on your own, free as a bird, and now you're back, an unwed mother with no support, more miserable than any of the neighborhood women.

What a load you've taken on, old girl! What are you hoping to gain, where do you think you'll get with all this?

It took me a while to earn the confidence of some very suspicious clients, almost all of them new to me.

What had become of my old girlfriends, the ones who'd protected me and helped raise me? Poor Suzy, for instance, who left to set up business in town as a barmaid, one night when she was really down, checked out of life's hotel with the help of some poison. And Lulu, plump and always full of fun, had wrecked her voice with alcohol and tobacco. It was pathetic to hear her singing her silly romantic tunes with a voice like sandpaper.

And the others had also started to age, which meant coming down a few notches and entering the category of cheap trick, but they hadn't given up, were still proud of their past, in spite of it all, but with such a fiery temper that few who paid them a visit ever returned for more.

Believe me, it took lots of patience and conniving to satisfy all those poor souls. They would pile on the insults something awful every time I missed a pleat or lost a button.

But what can I say, times were hard. Lots of men were out of work, which meant that the young fellows couldn't afford Sin Street as often as before. The women spent less and less on basic things like food, clothes, and of course, laundry. What else could they do, they had to keep tight

---

* Wooden sandals worn by women around the house and at the public baths, or *hammam*.

accounts if they didn't want to starve, or get evicted by the landlords, who rented those little stalls by the day.

I worked on credit, which is what did me in.

Whenever the "ladies" managed to lay their hands on some cash, you can imagine what they would spend it on first: rent, doctor's visits, the grocery bill. And if there was anything left after all that, they would think of poor Ninette.

But I was afflicted by the same dire straits, the worst of all: I was in debt.

The local loan shark was doing a brisk business, I can tell you that!

I don't know what race he descended from, but I'll bet he wasn't his father's son. A pig's head on a bull's body, a hairless face with the yellowed teeth of an old mule and the bulging belly of a woman nine months pregnant.

He would take anything: jewelry, clothes, copper kitchen utensils, hand-knotted rugs. And when you were late with your payments, you should have seen the way he'd come after you. First he'd threaten to auction off all your belongings. Of course, that wouldn't even begin to cover what you owed him, and you'd remain in hock for life.

He'd been in the neighborhood for an eternity, it seemed, like a horsefly that you can't get rid of, stuck to your skin, sucking your blood and sweat.

And how was my son doing amid this cast of characters, all this misery, amid the smoke from cheap restaurants, the lewd songs, the all-night partying among Greek fishermen back from some sponge-diving adventure?

Well, he grew up in spite of it all, like a weed up from between two paving stones.

In the early days, he really put me through my paces! He was insatiable, and I didn't have enough milk. He'd wake me up ten times a night with that screaming of his that sounded like a strangled cat. All the neighbors were up in arms, unable to sleep through the night. Imagining that I'd gone out for a walk or something, they'd get up on the upper terraces and scream over to me: hey, Ninette, your kid's crying. As if I didn't know it! Ninette was wide-awake and crying her eyes out over her fate.

Only someone who has known real misery knows what the word appetite means. And that son of mine would have eaten me raw if he could have. He was made of flesh and blood, and not out of cookie dough, like rich folks' kids. He wanted to live, to grow up, after all, and to join the ranks of the other poor people who were struggling.

I have to say I liked his spirit, because it came from my side of the family, not from his no-good jellyfish of a father.

But in the meantime, since I wasn't getting enough to eat myself, I didn't have enough milk to feed him. So I would trick him with some weak tea here, some water-soaked bread there. And I would sit him down on a little rug right in front of me while I washed a "lady's" dirty laundry. Why he didn't die of an infection, like so many others, still puzzles me. Because during the heat of the summer, when even adults had a hard time staying alive, so many city children would be carried away.

"Put him on a special diet," everyone told me, when he did finally get sick.

But he had been on a diet since the day he was born, poor lamb! No, my friends, my baby is dying of hunger. What he needs is a regular dose of milk, with just enough sugar, morning and evening, a nice bowl of baby cereal, the kind you see in drugstore windows and at fine grocers and that costs an arm and a leg.

I don't know how, but we managed to hobble along, and the days along with us.

The boy started growing up, lost his chubby little baby face and started getting long and thin. You should have seen his scrawny thighs, his stooped shoulders, his big dark eyes that took up half his face.

All day, he wandered from shop to shop, doing errands for the "ladies," sometimes getting slapped, sometimes getting candy and coins.

For the least little thing, I took it all out on the poor kid, all my frustration over the lack of work, of food, of everything. He got so used to beatings that he didn't even cry anymore. Instead, it was me who howled through my tears all the while I was hitting him, calling on the heavens and my neighbors as witness to my unhappy fate.

Whenever I got started, someone would come save the little one and preach to me about how to raise my son.

What really hurt was that he was becoming a petty thief and a liar. He would take anything within reach—money that I kept under the mattress, food I was keeping for dinner or the next day, whatever. And then with his I-didn't-do-it look, you'd have had a hard time convincing yourself he was guilty.

For the disappeared cake or the stewpot suddenly licked clean, you could maybe blame the alley cat or prowling dogs. A convenient explanation, at least. But when money starts vanishing, or an apple or an orange that a client gave me, where did all that get to, I wonder?

No sense beating around the bush. The thief came from inside the house, not outside. All I had to do was step outside for a second, and the deed was done.

"Just wait," I said to myself. "Next time, I'll make him pay dearly for this. All I'll need is a little shred of evidence, and then we'll see what we'll see."

One day, when I was downtown on some errand, I came back to find the whole neighborhood in revolt.

Around Lulu's little stall, all the women were gathered and shouting, for the landlord was trying to evict the poor tenant who couldn't pay that day's rent.

And yet Lulu swore to the heavens that she had put some money aside, under the mattress or the tablecloth—she couldn't remember which—a nice, shiny twenty-franc coin. Who could have taken it? She was gone for only a few seconds to go fill her water pitcher at the public fountain, and had left Ninette's son to keep watch.

How could a twenty-franc coin have disappeared into thin air? She was at her wits' end trying to come up with an answer.

When asked, Ninette's son just raised his hands in the air, and in his usual babble explained that he hadn't seen anything unusual. Then, frightened no doubt by all the hubbub, zip! He took off running.

Something flashed through my mind. My heart started pumping, and in a few strides, I was back home.

The boy was stretched out on the mattress and pretending to be asleep. But as soon as he saw me enter so suddenly, drop my bags noisily to the floor, and slam the door, he couldn't pretend any longer. He sat up and hopped out of bed, fearing what was coming. Instinctively, he sank his head into his shoulders and raised his arms in that defensive position of his.

His hangdog expression almost got the better of me, but instead, I let go with a wild, hoarse scream.

"It was you!"

"Mama, I won't do it again."

And the stolen coin fell from his open hand and clanged to the floor.

"It was you, you miserable thief, it was you!"

I was all over him, hitting and crying and hitting some more.

"Let me see the hand that did such an evil thing. This one? Here, take this, then!"

And I bit down as hard as I could. Now, I thought, every time you reach that hand out to take something that isn't yours, the scar will make you remember the bite, and maybe you'll think twice.

His scream of pain weakened my will.

Seeing him fall back, all pale, his hand bloody and bruised, I thought at first I'd killed him. Fear and remorse gave me the strength to open the door to the outside and call:

"Arrest me, I've killed my son. Arrest me, I'm a madwoman."

The neighbor women, Lulu and all the others, piled into the room.

Dazed and leaning against the wall to keep from falling over, I held out the coin.

It took only one look for everyone to understand what had just taken place.

So Lulu rushed to the boy, picked him up in her arms and smothered him in kisses, crying: hey, why did you want to do a naughty thing to

Mama and me? That rat of a landlord put me out in the street; where was I going to sleep tonight?

And then, as if suddenly inspired, to spare me the shame of having a thief for a son, she cried out:

"Wait, girls, it's not that he stole, it's that I gave him the coin to keep watch over. Believe me, I swear. How stupid can I get, Lord Almighty? Stupid and brainless! I'd completely forgotten. Come on, Ninette, cheer up and come give your son a hug. The rest of you, get moving and find me a clean handkerchief and some alcohol and some mercurochrome. We'll bandage him up nice and good, and tomorrow it won't even show.

I know it's none of my business, Ninette, but this little guy spends too much time hanging around the neighborhood. How old is he getting to be? Almost six? It's high time you got him to school. If it'll encourage you, I'll pay for his book bag if I can get a few good days in this week."

"And me, I'll buy him his lunchbox."

"And for his smock, go talk to the head of the local charity. Nice lady, she'll give you a pair of shoes, too. Go on, do it, Ninette, you'll thank us someday for our good advice."

And then they left us to ourselves.

The boy had stopped crying, but he shuddered from time to time. Was he shivering from cold or fear? I wanted to hold him in my arms, but he jumped to his feet and cowered against the wall, holding his arms up for protection: won't do it again, Mama, *pwahmise* I won't.

"Shush now, silly, you're breaking my heart. Don't be scared, Mama isn't going to hurt you anymore, I swear. Come over here and let me love you some. You've had your share of beatings, haven't you? *Pwahmise* you won't be a bad boy anymore, will you? You feel sorry for yourself and your dog of a mother, don't you? All we could cling to was the little pride we had left, and to live by the sweat of our brow. And then you wanted us to lose even that? Nothing left for us in that case but to go drown ourselves in the sea, son!

Listen to me, little one, and try to understand, even though what I'm going to say is over your head: I love you more than I could ever love anyone, myself included. You're my great love, my only hope. Walk a straight line in life, that's all I ask. Others will make mistakes, but not you, because you're you, fatherless child, son of crazy Ninette. Because you have no right, do you hear me, because you're not like everybody else. At the slightest little thing, they'll say: well sure, that was to be expected, the apple doesn't fall far from the tree!

Where does he come from? From Ninette, by God, and only from her. What the father ended up doing, and the father's father, I have no idea. I wouldn't even care if they turned out to be thieves. That's their business. As for this son, I'll see to it that he follows my morals, since he's mine.

Ninette was lots of things, but she was never a thief. No one, ever, can boast that he paid the full price of the suffering she was subjected to when she would sell herself for a crust of bread. Society owes me something, me, the unwed mother abandoned with a baby to feed.

So you're going to go to school as soon as you can, isn't that right, little sonny boy? Ah, just knowing that for eight hours a day you'll be away from this neighborhood, I already feel that we're halfway to salvation."

That's how I talked to my son that evening.

All night long, with his little wounded hand between my breasts, I held him on my knee and sang him the sweet songs of my grandmother.

A week later is when I came and presented him to you, Mr. Director, Sir. Six years ago, can you believe it? He was a wild child, a street kid from Sin Street, to put it bluntly. He gave you trouble at first, but your patience and goodness overcame his hardheadedness. It was never his fault, if he ever happened to do something wrong.

"Come now, Ninette, all that's in the past now. What you have today is a fine boy, obedient, respectful, mature beyond his years from everything he's had to endure. Vocational school will add the finishing touches by teaching him a trade, one that will put bread on the table, good bread, even, with all the extras—butter and jam—to make it that much tastier. I won't say we've turned your boy into some kind of wonder. But we have taught him everything an honorable and fair-minded person needs to know, taught him how to behave with himself and others."

For all that, Mr. Director, Sir, I thank you. And now, it's my turn to give you a piece of good news. You know what I've been striving for all these years, to go live on the avenue lined with palm trees, facing the bandstand? Well, the other day, I was just walking along, head down, mulling a million little things in my head. And suddenly, the director of the African Bank stops me in mid-step with these words:

"Well, hello there, Ninette."

"Good day to you, Sir," I answer back politely.

"Is it true, Ninette, that you've been left with a child who isn't yet old enough to work but who's learning a good trade at school?"

"That's right."

"And how are you managing in the meantime?"

"How am I managing? God only knows. I wash, I rinse, I mend, I iron, I do household chores."

"And where is it you're living?"

"Sin Street, Sir."

"That's not good, not good at all, because of your son, you understand."

The gentleman stopped and thought a moment, then said: "Listen, Ninette, if it's really true that you're on the straight and narrow for good, as I've heard tell, I'm going to set you up as concierge at my bank, with a place to live and such and such a monthly salary. You'll live there with that boy of yours. How does all that sound to you?"

"How does it sound? You're asking me how all that sounds? If I weren't worried you'd take it wrong, I'd give you a big kiss."

"You can have a day off for your son's bar mitzvah,* Ninette, and my wife will be a witness. Go now and pack up your house, and get moved in."

And that's where things stand now, Sir.

"Ninette, didn't I always tell you that sooner or later, all your grief would be rewarded in this life?"

---

* The original French uses the word "communion," but it can be assumed in this context to mean bar mitzvah, sometimes called "communion juive" in French.

"So the rabbi from Djerba was right, was he? Maybe, except for the matter of the Messiah. I've got a good mind to go tell him to change his sermon, and to use me as his example. Because the Almighty, he sends a Messiah to each and every one, without making us wait for years and centuries, until we're all dead and buried."

"Well done, Ninette. You and your son have put the worst behind you now. Pain, sorrow, shame, all that can be forgotten. And like good folks who love each other, you can move forward into a bright future. And look! There's a little sunshine just come out to brighten and warm your way. Good luck, Ninette, good luck!"

Sfax, October–December 1938

APPENDIX

A FLANEUR IN SFAX, 1918

Vitalis Danon had only recently arrived in Sfax when he penned this letter, in 1918, to the president of the Alliance Israélite Universelle. He was but twenty-one years old, newly graduated from the institution's Parisian teaching college, the École Normale Israélite Orientale. Danon's letter strikes an intimate tone, as did the letters of many teachers in that organization's employ. It reflects Danon's zeal for his chosen profession and his fascination as he explored Sfax for the first time. Meandering through the city, Danon observes it through the lens of Orientalist literature and art—his eyes are drawn to the winding streets, the "violent" colors of the open market, and the artisans (Jewish as well as Muslim) producing traditional crafts by hand. From the chaos of the city Danon retreats to his books and meditations. An avid reader with a self-described taste for the eclectic, Danon devoured French classical theatre (Pierre Corneille), romantic poetry (Alfred de Vigny), philosophy (Paul Janet), and novels—with a special mention of Gustave Flaubert, whose exoticizing historical fresco Salammbô (1862) inscribed Tunisia's place in the French Orientalist canon. Danon's letter itself might be read as a classic Orientalist tract, were it not for the complexity of his own identity and origins; as a fellow Mediterranean Jew, he was a product and protégé of the very civilizing mission he would offer his students.

Sfax, 27 June 1918
To the president of the Alliance

Mr. President,

In my previous reports, I had the pleasure of telling you something about my pupils. This time, I would ask that you kindly allow me to say a little about myself.

Was it my vocation to become a primary school teacher? I cannot really say. What I do know is that as soon as I was old enough to begin thinking about future choices, it was my single most important ambition. I seemed naturally disposed to follow this career path. Now that I think about it, I feel that I would have had trouble working in any other profession, since I do know something about, and am indeed fond of, the carpenter's and blacksmith's trades, the latter being that of my father, one of the Alliance's first apprentices in Adrianople [Edirne]. I would find other professions difficult not because of the fatigue involved—there are days when my work at school feels overwhelming, when I come home broken-spirited—but because no other line of work would allow me to engage my mind in intellectual pursuits in quite the way that the life of a schoolteacher does. Reading has become vital for my mind, as imperative as eating or sleeping for the body. But whether I am reading a newspaper or some book or other, I never quite forget my status of schoolteacher. And I am always on the lookout, so to speak, for good, simple readings that I can use in class or some idea I can develop with my pupils. We readily stop what we are doing in class just to talk. Or we take the longest possible route to get to the point, like the schoolboys that we are! Too bad if we don't get through all of the material; we don't have exams to take!

Outside school hours, I have to seek my own entertainment. For me, the big question is how not to be bored on Saturdays. There are no movie houses, no theaters. Actually, there is one movie house, but it shows only crime stories, the kind of movie I'm instinctively repelled by and would never go to see. But I do walk a great deal, and always find the same pleasure, the same unquenchable curiosity, when I stroll through the narrow, winding streets of the Arab quarter. I enjoy stopping to admire an oddly sculpted or painted door. No matter which direction you take, you always end up at the Arab markets. What are they, these Arab markets? A tangled succession of uneven streets, a row of shops no bigger than a cupboard, where hundreds of items are hung from the wall or spread out on floor mats, just waiting to be scooped up by the curious shopper. First there are the perfume stalls, with their tiny potbellied bottles of rose water, jasmine, and carnation essences lined up on shelves painted in picturesque pink and green. Together, they give off a heavy and complex scent, impossible to define, but distinctly Arab. Next is the dyers' street. Handwoven blankets, belts, saddlecloth, and carpets strung from one balcony to another. The colors are almost violently intense, but from a certain distance, the overall effect is striking, especially in full sunlight. You then need to retrace your steps, since the dyers' street is a cul-de-sac. Shade is provided by assembling what look like bedcovers or, more precisely, old flour sacks that have been stitched together and then strung up rather haphazardly above the street to create a kind of movable canopy that threatens to collapse with the slightest breeze. And then, among the heap of grocery shops that spill into the road, as you move among the sacks of fava beans and chickpeas, the slabs of bread and tubs of olives, you come across an ancient doorway. As soon as you pass through, you feel a burst of cool air settle around your shoulders like an icy cloak. You are now in one of the covered markets, the fabric souk. All that is rich and luxurious in the Arab way of life now spreads before you, a true delight for the eye: silks and satins, gold-embroidered costumes, sequined fabrics, sumptuous moirés. I stop and listen to some Arabs haggle over the price of a Gafsa carpet, picking up a word here and there in the flood of conversation, then continue on my way. Exiting through a doorway on the right, you land in the middle of the jewelers' souk. The Jewish jewelers, easily recognizable by the length of their beards and by their jet-black eyes that watch as you pass, are laboring over tiny anvils or chiseling chunky silver bracelets, as wide as napkin rings, so graceful with their arabesques and interlocking floral patterns. I pass quickly by the shoe-makers and blacksmiths, etc. You return somewhat weary from this trek through the uneven streets, a little ill at ease, where at times you have to hug the walls to yield passage to the native women who, in their voluminous white veils, look more like bundles of laundry waddling along, walking almost like living beings.

But I really feel good only when I'm at home. This is not to say that I always have my nose in a book. I also like to wander around, daydreaming, after a couple hours of serious reading. What do I mean by serious reading? You be the judge. My choices are eclectic; I move haphazardly from the works of Flaubert to those of G. Séailles or Paul Janet, from Vigny poems to a novel by Murger, Courteline, or Bourget, from Corneille to Paul Fort or Larmain. But this fondness for reading, a fondness that is almost a passion, will it abide forever? I fear getting bogged down in this dreadfully humdrum social scene I live in, where everyone acts out of sheer habit and is content to have a few paltry ideas now and then. For the moment, I am still independent-minded in thought and deed. I resist certain habits that society imposes. I would be curious to know what so many schoolteachers do, who turn away from reading and writing once they have obtained their teacher certification. I know some who delude themselves into thinking they can maintain a life of the mind by skimming a daily newspaper or paging through a magazine, to stay up on the latest, as they say.

Thinking, reflecting, dreaming. It's all so painful sometimes! Here in my moral isolation, a thousand questions flood my head. And I would especially like to know, though how can one ever really know, what the purpose of my life is. Why do I work, for whom? Will the passing years forge my ideal? But I know that I have moments of weakness; I have often wished I could stop thinking, just to find some peace. Stop thinking! Give up the fight? Shame on me, since life itself is a constant struggle!

This confession, Mr. President, might prove to you that I still have some energy deep inside to resist stagnation, the annihilation of thought, and that I still have a great passion for study. I hope that I shall always be worthy of the mission with which you have so honored me.

Yours sincerely,

Vitalis Danon

A VISIT TO THE JEWS OF DJERBA
(TRAVEL NOTES), 1929

During his years as an AIU director and teacher, Danon penned a number of socio-logical and anthropological essays in addition to his fiction. This travelogue, pub-lished in 1929, describes his visit to the island of Djerba, home to one of the oldest Jewish communities of North Africa and the Middle East. Danon travels to Djerba with a head full of myths; once on the island, he is startled, seemingly in equal mea-sure, by the poverty and hospitality of his Jewish hosts. To Danon, Djerba's Jews seem untouched by time, the "illustration of scenes straight out of the Bible." This record of his encounter is less troubling than that of his later visit to Gabès, and he leaves already nostalgic for Djerba's simplicity. His is not an encounter with peers, however, but with a people he views as archaic, arrested in another time—a reminder of his sense of the relative superiority of Western ways.

A Visit to the Jews of Djerba
(Travel Notes)
To my friends Jean and Lysa Jivré

I

On the North African coast, off the far southern tip of Tunisia's east-ern shoreline, lies a flat, sandy island, just barely off the mainland. The large Jewish population living there claims ancestry dating back to King Solomon. It is the island of Djerba, the celebrated Meninx, Island of the Lotus-Eaters, where adverse winds blew Ulysses and his men off course and onto land.

From Homer to the present, how many travelers have sung the praises of the island's mild climate and enchanting groves! Others, smit-ten with Orientalism, have lovingly described the simple life of the local Arabs scattered among the island's seven small villages. But as for me, I boarded the small sailboat that carried me on the final leg of my journey from Sfax to Djerba knowing my only reason for going was to visit the island's Jews.

I lived a week of feverish anticipation prior to departure. The sonorous name of Djerba played continuously in my mind like a haunting refrain: Djerba! Djerba! I'll finally get to see it, that island lost and reconquered time and again!

Countless populations landed there, hoping to lay the foundations of an unassailable empire. They blew in and out like the wind and the sand. And of its conquerors—the Carthaginians, the Romans, the Barbary pirates, the knights of Rhodes, the counts of Tripoli, the Norman warriors of the kingdom of Sicily, the Spanish, the Turks—nothing remains.* All have disappeared. And by some feat of the will, under the boot of however many successive oppressors, this usually recalcitrant people submitted, kept their heads down, allowing no humiliation to weaken their unshakable faith. And since they believed in miracles, a miracle happened. Once the sky had cleared, the Jews raised their heads and went on living.

This is what was going through my head as I made my way, by night, through the labyrinth of dark, narrow streets, to the quay of Sfax's canal.

On the dock next to the sailboat, whose shape we could just barely make out, a handful of passengers were chattering among themselves. A whistle blew, bringing conversation to a halt, and we hastened to embark. The anchor was hoisted aboard, making a creaky, rusty noise, the sails were raised, and we glided ever so slowly among the other moored craft, and finally out to sea.

It was as if the sea was sleeping. We could barely feel its broad, sluggish undulations as they gently rocked us from port to starboard. A short while later, however, the wind picked up, the triangular sails fluttered, deployed in the increasingly stiff breeze, ballooned finally by a steady wind.

The red and white beacons lining the channel cast a trembling glow onto the dark water, and the moon, in turn, shone through a tear in the cloud layer. In the far distance before us, the horizon glowed dimly: we were sailing now on a silver sea.

---

* Nothing or almost nothing. There remains on the shore a Spanish castle that winds and sea air have nearly reduced to a ruin. (Author's footnote.)

It was a hot night, one of those stifling African nights when sleep eludes you, when body and spirit are overcome by the heat and humidity so typical of Tunisia in September, and that descend from the heavens as the sun sinks in the west.

An Arab from the south started singing one of those interminable nasal melodies, which everyone sitting around him intoned in unison as a refrain at the end of each stanza. Rocked by the rhythm of this strange monotonous chant, they were soon fast asleep right there on the deck. The last cigarette extinguished, the final coughs hushed, an airy silence reigned over this human flock as it slumbered. . . . Still, all night long, one little girl curled up against her mother was kept awake by a fit of coughing that the damp air was certainly making worse.

Unable to sleep on the hard planks, impatient to reach my journey's destination, I paced up and down the deck for a long while. To our right, a light appeared and disappeared at regular intervals. This was the Thyna lighthouse, built on the shore of ancient Thaenae, a Roman city now entirely buried beneath the sand. Thaenae was an important trade hub, as witnessed by traces of roads leading to Tripolitania, Tebessa, and Carthage. And by the light of the moon, as our vessel cut lazily through the compliant waves, I thought back to the time of dusty trade routes, the slow pace of caravans that transported immense treasures of pure ivory, colorful carved gems, amber and musk, fresh olives still full of oil, translucent dates. . . .

Dawn, at last.

"Where are we?" I asked someone, randomly.

"We're now in the waters off Djerba," answered an Italian, scanning the horizon.

"But there's nothing out there," I countered.

"Be patient, the sun will soon burn off the layer of haze that hangs above the water."

And as promised, after a while, in the distance, a flat land mass appeared, as the harbor lights blinked out, one after the other.

Everyone pressed toward the bow, gaze fixed on the shore, whose outline was coming more sharply into view.

Anyone who has sailed into an oriental port will recognize the bustling scene. Baggage handlers dressed in tatters rush up to passengers and snatch their luggage. And in loud, colorful language seconded by broad hand gestures, they get the message across that we are to follow them.

And follow I did. Upon leaving the marina, we were soon walking along a superb avenue lined with rushes.

Cube-shaped houses rose on either side of our route. In under a quarter of a mile, a white city rose into view, the classic Arab town with horizontal roofs alternating with domes, looking oddly like a cemetery for giants, each structure walled in by cactus and aloe. The surrounding countryside is nothing but gardens bristling with date palms, reaching their slender silhouettes to the sky. Olive trees and still more olive trees, some pruned into parasols, others all knotty and stunted, grove upon grove set against the yellow, furrowed soil, extend as far as the eye can see. The long straight alleys they create begin at my feet and meet at the horizon's vanishing point. But by now, my eyes are too tired to follow the looming horizon, and everything goes blurry. At a distance, you no longer distinguish the trees, with their powerful trunks and gray foliage. You see nothing but a greenish sea with silvery reflections, where the crests wave in the passing breeze.

Ah, if only I had turned on my heel and gotten right back on the boat that brought me here! For if I had, I would have kept locked in my memory the pastoral image of an incomparable African landscape.

But I kept walking, and after I had gone through a few vaulted lanes and come out onto the market square, I stopped in my tracks, disappointed. What spread before me was the poorest, most common southern village, with its clusters of wretched nomads, merchants squatting on the ground selling their unappetizing meats, goatskins of oil, sieves, and secondhand military uniforms. The town crier was walking his bicycle from group to group. Crowds would part as camels ambled through, preceded by a few sheep.

So this was the isle of golden sands, the enchanted Island of the

Lotus-Eaters? Who will give me a taste of lotus flower to make me forget such an unsightly display?

Standing there taking in the sights and sounds of the Arab market, I nearly forgot that I had come especially to see the Jews of Djerba.

So I wandered through the souks, taking little alleyways that often dead-end without warning, or crisscross in unexpected ways, forming a mind-boggling maze.

Ah, there they are! The Jews are recognizable by their black or dark-blue turbans, their baggy trousers and long shirts. They all go sockless in old, worn-out slippers. Everyone is dressed in clothing so tattered and miserable that you wonder if it was ever new.

Today, the weekly market day, they've all come out from the *hara*, from both the big and little ghettos, on foot, by donkey or bicycle, to buy and sell. How will they do on this day? They have no idea. But the God of Israel, great and almighty, has never abandoned his children. Which is why, his soul at peace after a lengthy dawn prayer, his stomach warmed by a tiny shot of alcohol, his pack on his back and his pocket jingling with change, the Djerbian Jew zigzags through the souk, on the alert for deals, hands and body in perpetual motion. He stops in front of a mound of wheat grain, stoops to take a handful, feels its weight, and then lets it flow back through his fingers like golden rainfall. The Bedouin names his price, then watches warily as his customer feigns disinterest. A few more of his fellow Jews join in the bargaining, and soon three or four are haggling loudly all at once, shouting and screaming, hurling insults and swearing by the living God and the Torah.

The storm suddenly dissipates, and our Hebrew brothers abandon the wheat and its Bedouin vendor to descend on a woman making the rounds with a basket of eggs, a pair of fowl, some items of jewelry, and a woolen blanket. And the bargaining resumes until one of them outbids the competition by a few pennies and gets the goods from the dazed woman, who hardly knows which way to turn.

Midday. The sun at its zenith beats down ruthlessly upon the white city. The market's hustle and bustle has died down. The vast square where, moments ago, vendors were still noisily peddling their wares is now slowly emptying. Blind water carriers are still offering thirsty customers a drink for a penny or two. Bedouins and Arabs slake their thirst by drinking straight from the jug, lips stuck to the spout, head thrown back. But the Jew, obsessed as he is with cleanliness, grabs one of his long shirttails that hang over his trousers and places it over the spout as a makeshift water filter.

Ah, those trademark shirttails that make it so easy to distinguish Jew from Arab, so ugly and so filthy, are used for just about everything: to wipe sweat off the brow, to dust off a place to sit on the sidewalk, or to carry home the gooey dates and fresh vegetables just purchased! And if you enter into one of those smoky, den-like eateries, you'll see men, young and old alike, wiping their hands on their shirttails, a perfectly normal gesture, while muttering a prayer before digging into their meal.

What an unforgettable experience it is to visit this street full of restaurants where Jews of all social ranks, dark-skinned musicians, and beggars congregate at all hours of the day! In front of one establishment, someone has lined up little round loaves of bread on low stools. A huge caldron of some nasty-looking stew is boiling away atop a stone hearth, and next to that, fish is grilling over tepid embers. An elderly man is kneeling over the coals that are smothered in dripping fat. He blows on them to keep them alive, swelling the veins in his neck, while his eyes water from the acrid smoke.

It is in this rutted street that I witness a most pathetic spectacle: an old one-eyed shoeshine man! On market days, assorted cobblers, being too poor to afford renting a stall, set up shop in the open air, stitching and patching dilapidated slippers, and hammer away at worn-out soles. A few steps further, tinsmiths sit on the uneven ground and work at turning old tin cans into oil lamps or coffeepots.

Set around the square of a caravansary, where kneeling camels chew their cud while nearby donkeys roll in the dust, the Jewish blacksmith shops open, forming a honeycomb of golden light. A glow emanates from deep within each, like a beacon in the dark of night, and you can just make out the blackened faces of the workers and their torsos barely covered in ragged shirts. The rest of the body recedes into the smoke. Hammers beat out the rhythm of the blacksmith's song. At every pause in the pounding, you can hear the asthmatic wheezing of the bellows. Outside the shop, the ground is strewn with rusty sickles and plowshares, latches, bits of grillwork, and other items typical of a scrap-metal junk heap, lined up against the outside wall in the sun. Someday, in response to some customer's urgent demand, the blacksmith will go and fish out a few pieces from the pile, a plowshare or a screen, heat them over the flame and beat them into shape as best he can.

II

Djerba is the kind of place that has remained impermeable to modern civilization. No cafés, no movie theaters, no dance halls. Not even the ubiquitous "Hôtel de France" or "Hôtel de l'Oasis" that you're sure to find in even the most remote African backwater. Happy is the land where hospitality is still shown in the old-fashioned way, when all you need to do if you are looking for a place to spend the night is to knock on anyone's door!

"Hello. Here is a letter for you from so-and-so, your relative. He's a friend of mine. I'm here from Tunis for a visit."

"Come right in! My house is yours, make yourself at home!"

And with that, a cluster of dark-eyed children, their sidelocks* spiraling out from under their skullcaps, gathers around to welcome me, calling out to their mother. The hostess, full of grace and reserve, hand extended but eyes lowered, moves slowly toward me, her impressive jewelry clinking with every step: silver wrist cuffs, heavy necklaces, and ankle bracelets in the Bedouin style make her look like a bejeweled idol.

It is in their inner courtyard, open to the sky, paved in floral tiles, that I am received, and soon surrounded by soft, dark eyes. They take me up to the rooftop terrace, from which one can discover the entire Jewish vil-

---

* Danon refers, here, to *peyot*, sidelocks worn by observant Jewish boys and men in deference to the Biblical injunction (Leviticus 19:27) against shaving the "corner" [*pe'ah*] of the head.

lage, the forest of olive trees, and the sea in the distance. Night is falling, but up there, everything is so beautiful and clear! Wide splashes of vermilion still paint stripes across the western horizon; above our heads, the sky is such a tender pink that you want to feel its softness to the touch. Down below, in the neighboring streets and alleyways, sounds of the early evening reach our ears, those noises peculiar to Arab towns that seem to come to life only at nightfall, as the men are returning from the souk.

I go down to mix with the groups that are making their way home, unrushed, as if the passage of time meant nothing to them.

The archaic silhouettes of passersby, the way they stand and move with such grace, the bearing of the veiled women as they sway beneath their silky mantles, everything here gives the illusion that the past is not dead and gone, but that life continues as in the ancient time of the Land of Canaan or the splendors of Zion. The thousand little tableaux that make up daily family life constitute a living illustration of scenes straight out of the Bible.

But how illusory is it, really? At this blessed hour when the first stars begin to twinkle, when the world melts into twilight, a local elder with the beard of a patriarch is sitting on the stoop in front of his immaculately white house. Is this not Abraham awaiting his guests? And to complete the scene, here's the pure oval face of Sarah peering from inside the half-open door.

And further down the street, who is that lovely young girl beneath her veils? She's looking over a low wall and seems to be watching for someone. It is the beloved of The Song of Solomon, brought back to life for the delight of our eyes and hearts.*

Night has fallen now, and the powdery pink that dusted the sky has faded to deep blue. This is no time to turn in for the night—My God, no!—bewitched as I am by the undefinable enchantment of this magic hour. Arabs on donkeys, their bells jingling in the dusk, ride up the main street that divides the Jewish village in two, followed closely by their

---

* Also known as the Song of Songs, the Song of Solomon, the fifth book of the Hebrew Bible, is replete with sexual language, image, and metaphor.

flocks. But a murmur suddenly rises above the tinkling bells and bleating sheep. Curious, I press on. And suddenly, around a corner, there appears the startling sight of a few dozen Jews standing with their arms crossed over their chests, faces lifted to the new moon, which they are blessing. A few steps away is the humble synagogue, its doors wide open, allowing me a glimpse into the interior, dimly lit by flickering oil lamps. . . .

Their lunar hymn swells, crescendoes, and dies away into the peaceful fields. Not a single night bird's call, not even a wisp of breeze disturbs the ceremony that unfolds at an even tempo. All around, the olive trees seem to stand still, as if in awe of the scene's majesty.

The faithful pray fervently, and this poignant setting in all its simplicity sends me deep into the past, as I relive those ancient Jerusalem nights when Israel reigned.

Eyes still full of sleep, the child is coaxed awake by his mother and rises to accompany his father to synagogue. Many faithful are already gathered, wrapped in their talliths [prayer shawls], some seated, others standing, all shouting at the top of their lungs, arms and eyes raised to the heavens, beseeching them to bear witness to the woes of Israel and and its acts of contrition.

With the last verses mumbled on the way out, practically in the street, we return home for a quick breakfast. The father heads for the souk and the child for the synagogue again, which is where he will spend his waking hours until his wedding day. He'll be there dawn to dusk, day in and day out, rain or shine, wind or searing sirocco. Sitting on mats in brotherly communion with sixty other boys of all ages, he will learn, as best he can, everything from the basic alphabet to commentaries on the Bible and the Talmud. Even on Saturdays, while the father is enjoying a long siesta, and the mother is sitting out front chatting with her neighbors, he goes back to synagogue to recite the Psalms, Proverbs, and Ecclesiastes. . . . Some of the elders are lulled to sleep by the monotonous drone of the boys' pious recitation.

The years go by, marked by the regular return of holidays and seasons. The child is growing strong and vigorous. His dear sidelocks corkscrew around his ears, and his untucked white shirt makes him look like a little man. Later, and with the help of the Almighty, he will grow into one of the pure glories of the Hebrew people, a jewel in the crown of Israel, for he has already memorized all the prayers, the Torah, and the hagiographies. He reads the Talmud, from the tractate of the egg to the tractate on divorce. He now knows what is permitted and what is forbidden. His rabbi has boldly opened the boy's eyes to the mysteries and vagaries of marriage: levirate, *agunah*, etc.* But when it comes to the history of other peoples of the world, or the history of his own ancestors, for that matter, he knows nothing; he is kept in the dark. Bible and Talmud, Talmud and Bible. Beyond these, all science is vain and tainted. . . .

Around the age of sixteen, when a downy shadow begins to darken his adolescent cheeks, the son is taken by his father to the souk to initiate him into the world of "business." Soon after, he is married to a young girl who, like the flowers of Africa that bloom and fade in one day, will suffer the ravages of multiple pregnancies and live like a slave in her own home. For example, the wife will sort and grind her own wheat. Awake before dawn, she kneads the bread dough, which she will then take to the neighborhood's communal oven, carrying the unbaked loaves on a plank balanced on her head. Whether rich or poor, all women suffer the same plight: they cook, do laundry, draw water from the well; they never take their meals at the table, but sit in the kitchen or out in the courtyard on a mat, long after the husband and children have gone to bed.

The family often grows larger, and the finances of the breadwinner fail to keep pace. When that happens, the father packs his bags and sets off for the big city: Sfax, Sousse, or Tunis, trusting that God will provide.

Living on bread and olives, he plies his trade, be he a jeweler, shoe-

---

* Hagiographies, or narratives praising religious figures, developed as a genre in Hebrew in the sixteenth century; some sections of the Bible might also be understood as hagiographic. The Talmud is the compendium of Jewish oral law and its elucidation. Danon also refers to specific Talmudic debates, including the question of whether one is allowed to eat an egg laid on a holy day; whether the brother of a married man must wed his deceased brother's widow (a levirate marriage); and under what circumstances an *agunah*, or abandoned wife, is allowed to remarry.

maker, grocer, dyer, tinsmith, or rabbi. He sleeps in his shop and washes his own clothes, mending them when needed. A penny at a time, spending next to nothing, he hoards whatever he earns. Through effort and privation, he turns a modest enterprise into a real business. It is then you'll hear him day and night invoking *Hakadosh barukh hu* [The Holy One, blessed be he].

He returns to Djerba only on major holidays. Just enough time to see his family, who have been staying with the grandparents in his absence, and he's back on the road again.

After three or four years, once he's become an established and reputable merchant or tradesman, he has his family join him in the city. The memory of his native land begins to fade. And should you be so thoughtless as to ask him about his island home, that most delightful corner of the world, forgetting the long white shirttails, the synagogue, and the schoolmaster's switch, he'll answer you with utter contempt: "Djerba? Oh yes, that place. It's full of savages!"

But fortune, alas, does not smile on everyone. And those who do not manage to succeed while in exile, despite prayer and penny-pinching, find themselves returning to the island. And if they are unable to make the market circuit, to forge iron implements or pound used tin into coffeepots, these returnees settle into some menial task at the synagogue, as rabbi or teacher.

Time for me to get back on the boat for Sfax. I'm suddenly overcome with emotion, despite my best efforts to hold back the tears. In this tiny, forgotten corner of the universe, I experienced such full days, in such a calm and peaceful atmosphere, that the very thought of returning to the city is terribly distressing.

Is it the limpid air, the incomparably mild climate, that I'll miss? Is it the carpet of olive groves and fruit trees that covers the island from one end to the other? Perhaps. But certainly the idea of leaving behind these lovely island-dwellers who have welcomed me as a brother is what pains me most deeply.

"Come back and see us next year!"

"May you stay in good health until then!"

I promise to return, with a wave of a hand, a smile, and a glimmer in the eye, but I know it will never happen. Life is a whirlwind that will snatch me up and set me down elsewhere, on other shores, where again I will have to make new friends only to leave them behind.

We shake hands one last time, I cast a final look out at the port and almost imperceptibly, we slide along the water that is so still that the boats and sails are reflected back.

As we pull away, the island grows increasingly distant, and soon disappears altogether into the blue horizon. . . .

MISSION TO GABÈS, 1937

An ancient Mediterranean town, the southern Tunisian city of Gabès was home to a centuries-old Jewish community by the time Danon visited in 1937. Danon's ambition was to obtain support from Gabès's rabbinical leadership for the establishment of an Alliance Israélite Universelle school there—a prerequisite, for the AIU, for its sponsorship of a new institution. Danon arrived in Gabès as an emissary of French Republicanism and Jewish liberalism, and his perspective on the local community reflects both his ambition and his prejudice. In his eyes, Gabès's Jews are isolated, poor, persecuted, and ignorant; its rabbi an overstuffed and unyielding traditionalist detached from his community and blindly invested in religious education; and the community as a whole a miniature and diluted version of the ancient Jewish community of the island of Djerba, located just ninety kilometers south of Gabès and long the source of Gabès's religious leadership.

Sfax, 24 September 1937
TO: The Alliance Israélite Universelle
FROM: Vitalis Danon
SUBJECT: Mission to Gabès

Mr. President,

You did me the honor of entrusting me with exploring the possibility of opening a school in Gabès. I waited until the Sukkot holidays to travel there, since that is when the Jews of the south, usually scattered among several surrounding villages to conduct their business, return to the city for some time off with their families.[*]

The road between Sfax and Gabès—137 kilometers—cuts through the countryside in a straight line running parallel to the Mediterranean. For the first thirty or forty kilometers, you see nothing but gardens and

---

[*] A harvest festival, Sukkot commemorates the forty years in which the biblical Israelites wandered in the desert after their exodus from Egypt. The holiday is celebrated by feasting in temporary shelters (sukkot, singular sukkah) akin to those that might have been used by the wandering tribes.

olive groves, Sfax's green belt. Then all of a sudden, with no transition, you are in a desert plain. The sand is dazzlingly white. In fact, everything is white: the land, the sky, the sun, the woolen burnouses* worn by the locals, the cubic houses where only the door provides a little rectangle of green in the otherwise total whiteness.

Eighty kilometers, and more desolation, scorched earth, deep ravines cut by *oueds*† born of sudden downpours, short-lived rivers that flow violently for mere minutes before disappearing into the desert sands. Then suddenly, blotting out the sea, there appears a dark green spot on the horizon, the oasis of Gabès. It extends lengthwise, looking like a scarf tossed across the beach.

There is something so unexpected about coming upon living nature once again in the midst of a desert that one forgets the fatigue and monotony of the road.

We get closer and closer, and are finally there. The ribbon of road winds around hundreds of secret gardens, and runs along a creek so tranquil that it seems to be sleeping beneath the abundance of vegetation that blossoms all around. The creek starts to widen and to look more like a river, deep in some places, flowing under a modest little footbridge, beneath which young Arabs swim naked. They play at splashing each other, laughing and shouting and dancing.

But where are the little Jewish children? Back in their own neighborhood. They take care not to go play in the water: they would be pummeled with stones. So they glumly play at home in the dusty alleys outside their doors. They will never experience the joys of swimming in a flowing creek, or taking part in donkey races in the palm grove. They will remain prisoners of the filthy backstreets of the Jewish quarter where disorganized municipal services come to collect the garbage only when they are in the mood to do it, and sweep the streets willy-nilly, without watering them down first to settle the dust.

---

* A burnous, or burnoose (from the Arabic *burnus*), is a long cloak made of coarse wool, worn by Arabs and Berbers across North Africa.

† Danon uses the French spelling of the Arabic word *wad*, meaning dry riverbed.

Here, we come upon a group of children. They swim gleefully atop a sand pile. A few of them, as if taken by surprise at my arrival, stand stock-still and stare with their dark eyes. I gesture to them not to be afraid and beg them not to run away.

I must admit they are quite an amusing sight in their little bouffant pants, their burnouses worn over their heads against the sun, and their little red skullcaps.

"Hello, boys," I say. "I'm a schoolteacher, a Jew like you. Let's go over here in some shade and have a chat, shall we?"

A little wary at first, they soon warm to my presence, and each one tells me his name. And they start talking about the non-Jewish school that some of them attend, about the *kuttab*,* and about the rabbi.

Let me first say a few words about the lay of the land in Gabès.

Imagine if you will two very long parallel streets running from the beach all the way to the countryside, joined together by little parallel side streets, creating a ladderlike grid stretching across the sand for more than two kilometers.

The well-to-do Jews live along one of these long streets, in what is called Gabès-town. There is a school here that, since its earliest days, has been attended by only Jewish children.

At the far end of Gabès-town, there is a Jewish quarter, Djara, and some ways further, the road runs right into the desert. Vacant lots are scattered with refuse, garbage thrown into ditches or onto mounds. Not a single tree, no streets or roads, nothing but a winding beaten path. This is Menzel, a village in ruins where only the most wretched live out their days. I'll refrain from further description. When it comes to sheer misery and filth, there could exist nothing worse.

And yet, it is at the entrance into Menzel that, for whatever reason, the state decided to build a very costly school, the most beautiful one I have had occasion to see in all of Tunisia.

In 1935, Jewish pupils were chased out of Gabès-town and Djara and

---

* The *kuttab* (or *kouttab*) is the primary-level Koranic school.

told they could go to school in Menzel, where three classrooms were ready for them.

To fully understand the tragedy of this situation for these pupils, you have to make the trip on foot out of Gabès-town and out to Menzel. Four times a day, in winter when the wind blows so hard you can hardly breathe, let alone walk upright, or beneath the baking sun from March through early fall.

My little friends and I walked the whole way from Gabès-town to Menzel, very tiring for their little legs. By my calculations, in winter, you would have to get up at six o'clock to make it to school in time for class (7:45). Remember that these little ones also go first to the synagogue in the morning, and then there are always a few chores to be done around the house, not to mention breakfast, which isn't always ready. At eleven, they go back home, and leave for school again around one. And at four in the afternoon, deliverance at last. But not yet, since to go back through town they will have to do battle with the little Arab children who pelt them with stones from behind the cemetery walls.

The little Jewish pupils returned home more than once with wounds and injuries. The civil authorities did send a police officer to protect the children on their way home. That lasted about a week. Deal with it on your own, was their answer.

Parents wrote letter after letter to the Human Rights League, to Chautemps, to Herriot, to Jean Zay, to the Resident General, to the Board of Education, but got no response.* Their protests fell on deaf ears.

Two years have gone by. The Arabs have grown more insolent than ever, and the Jews have lost their will, and no longer know to how to react.

This is what the Jewish pupils explained to me, in the clearest and simplest terms.

---

* Camille Chautemps and Édouard Herriot both served as French prime ministers during this period, and Jean Zay as the French Minister of National Education and Fine Arts. The "Resident General" refers to the official representative of the French government in Tunisia during the protectorate. At the time of Danon's writing in 1937, the position was held by Armand Guillon.

I next pay a visit to the chief rabbi, after having my calling card delivered to the president of the Community.* I find the rabbi settled comfortably under the sukkah, sitting on a carpet surrounded by a mound of pillows. It is not yet noon, but while waiting for lunchtime he is taking a little nap. Never in my life have I seen such a corpulent, muscular, well-fed rabbi. He is a giant of a man, the very picture of health, and I do believe that if, on some whim, he were ever to enter a boxing ring, he would knock out his opponent in a single blow, just one would do.

He dresses the way they do in Djerba: a white, puffy-sleeved shirt, baggy trousers in the Zouave style, and an enormous black turban on his almost beast-like head. It must take quite a solid neck to support such a heavy edifice! His deep black hair and salt-and-pepper beard grow untamed like vines in a virgin forest, and nearly obscure his bloated face.

But those eyes, equally black, sparkling, full of irony and mischief, with an insistent, indiscreet gaze that registers your every detail, turns you inside out. The windows to the soul!

Barefooted, the rabbi is now sitting cross-legged, a large checkered handkerchief spread over his knees. From deep inside one of his shirt pockets, he withdraws a snuffbox. He takes a sizable amount between his thumb and index, and inserts it between the inside of his cheek and his gums. He performs this little operation without the slightest hint of embarrassment. And why should he be embarrassed, after all? Some smoke, others drink, and he takes snuff, in his own particular way.

"The Alliance Israélite, that's out of Paris, isn't it? Yes, I know all about it, and everything you say is quite true; it's OK, but it's really just for big cities. What good would it do here? And who are these folks in Gabès anyway? They're all Jews from Djerba, the fortress, the refuge for the Torah, and where tradition is still respected in its purest form like nowhere else. So, as soon as Djerba gets its Alliance school, Gabès will follow."

The rabbi seems aloof, distant, detached. What's the use of getting all excited over an issue as futile as secular schooling?

* Here and in what follows, the "Community" refers to the *kahal*, the executive board or community council of the Jewish community of Gabès.

"But rabbi, what about the children who have stones thrown at them every day by Arab boys? And the fatigue of the walk to school? Eight kilometers a day, rabbi, summer and winter, shouldn't that be taken into account?"

"Persecution? You know very well that such things are to be expected. Are we not in *galut*, in exile? How would God make us feel it otherwise? When the Messiah comes, if it pleases the Almighty . . ."

But people have started arriving in the sukkah. The rabbi extends his hand, and both young and old jostle to kiss it in fervent devotion.

Everyone sits down. An elder explains the reason for his visit: this young man here wants to marry my daughter, God willing. So, awaiting the official ceremony, could you write us out a little contract?

The rabbi picks up an old envelope lying about on a table, turns it over and jots down a few notes. Then, on a sheet of school workbook paper, he draws up the contract. He raises his head and says: listen now. The son of so-and-so commits to marrying the very gracious virgin, daughter of such-and-such, in accordance with the following conditions: the future wife will bring as dowry a complete bedding set—including a woven coverlet from Gafsa, jewelry as befits the father's honor, and brass utensils for the ritual bath. In exchange for which, the future husband will write out a ketubah, a written promise to his future wife of such-and-such amount of money. The rabbi extends his pen to the parties in agreement, and they sign, followed by more hand-kissing and niceties.

Next in line is a Jewish merchant from Sfax who, in order to get around some onerous fees at the goyim court,* appeals to the rabbi for help. Here is the story: a Jew from Gabès has failed to keep up with his installment payments. Would the rabbi reason with him?

But it's already noon, and the rabbi needs to have his lunch. His children, all sturdy and chubby-cheeked, their white shirts worn over baggy trousers, are now all busying themselves in the sukkah. On a glazed

---

* The "goyim court," or "non-Jewish court," might refer to a state court, a consular court, or a shari'a (Islamic law) court. In Tunisia, as elsewhere in North Africa and the Middle East, Jews brought legal cases to all of these courts, as befitted their various interests and the case involved.

ceramic platter, a mountain of dates and pomegranates is brought in. A mat is rolled out on the floor for the women who, considered to be impure, cannot sit at the table with men.

I make a discreet exit, having obtained the rabbi's promise that he will hold a meeting the next day in the synagogue with the Community leaders.

.   .   .

The Jews of Gabès originally came from all over: Tripoli, Tunis, Algiers. But the bulk of the population is from Djerba. If you want to live the Jewish life from two thousand years ago, then Djerba is the place, even more so than Palestine itself. This flat little island, halfway between Tunisia and Tripoli, has remained fiercely shut off from the outside world, and the many Jewish families are too numerous to count. And since the land has practically no resources, emigration becomes a necessity, so that everywhere in Tunisia, from north to south, the country's other Jewish communities have undergone a veritable invasion of Jews from Djerba. The wealthiest families of Tunis, the famous lawyers and doctors, are descendants of former emigrants from that island.

Extremely thrifty, living on a bowl of boiled chickpeas and a handful of dates, often sleeping in attics, thanks to this life of hard work and sacrifice, the Jews of Djerba have managed to carve out an enviable niche for themselves in commerce.

And if your bad luck causes commercial success to pass you by, you need not worry. Just become a rabbi! For the Bible, the Torah, and the Talmud are learned at the mother's breast. They've got it written into their bone marrow! So, there is not a Jewish community, large or small, that does not have its Djerbian rabbi.

.   .   .

The Jews of Gabès who are originally from Tunis or Algeria, who have come from up north and have had more contact with modern life, are quite distinct from their fellow Jews from the south. The northerners, often merchants, professionals, and military officers, in frequent contact with the European population, have slowly become assimilated, in the pejorative sense of the word, since they allow their daughters to marry goyim, officers, and functionaries.

This is not at all to say that they have lost contact with Jewish life. They feel a kind of raw sympathy toward their fellow Jews from Djerba and would like very much to help raise their standard of living. These more sophisticated Jews, who see things from above and at a distance—since they are not involved in the community's day-to-day affairs—have provided me with detailed accounts of the people's suffering.

The tax on kosher meat brings in, at most, forty thousand francs a year, and apartment rentals add another twenty to twenty-three thousand, when all units are occupied, which almost never happens. Apart from that, there is little other income. None, in other words.

And yet, the chief rabbi and his assistant, who are remunerated and housed, cost this impoverished Community thirty thousand francs. Not to mention the three other rabbis that "absorb" the income from the synagogue. It's gotten to the point where—and I was able to observe this with my own eyes—there is not a cent left, absolutely nothing, to even give the synagogue a new coat of whitewash.

Every year, on two different occasions, the chief rabbi goes back home for personal business. And since there is always a couple that needs counseling or some religious issue to be dealt with, he entrusts his assistant with his seal and his authority. Between the two of them, they eat up half of the revenue meant for the Charity Fund.

Gabès does not have a state-funded regional hospital. So when indigent Jews are sick they depend on the Community to pay their medical expenses. Add to that the expenses involved in the lodgings, upkeep, and return fare for fellow Jews passing through.

Elderly rabbis on a quest, fake rabbis in need of a holiday, charlatans, and amulet vendors, everything that North African Jewry produces by way of wandering souls seems to pass through Gabès at some point or another.

Gabès, after all, is only thirty kilometers from the tomb of the miraculous Rabbi Yossef el Maarabi, near the Roman baths of El Hamma, where sufferers of various ailments or rheumatism go for their yearly cure. You are also just a short sailboat ride away from the holy community of Djerba, with its ancient synagogue, El Ghriba. There is also an Italian boat that makes a regular stop in Gabès on its way down to Tripoli. If you leave Gabès at midnight, you're in Tripoli by dawn. And from there, after a short stay, another boat takes you to Alexandria. Alexandria! That's just a short trip away from Palestine!

The pilgrim down on his luck whines, complains, threatens, and even prays so much that the Community, having tired of supporting him yet eager to be rid of this scourge that goes begging in the cafés of the European neighborhoods, ends up pooling together enough money to pay for his "visa" to move on. And the city then breathes a sigh of relief. May God grant that he be the last of the wanderers. But no, as soon as one is gone, two others replace him. Sometimes an entire family with a sick child will make the journey all the way from deep in the Moroccan hinterlands.

All of this represents a huge expense for the tiny Community of Gabès, and the weight of it is crushing.

. . .

People here often recall the arrival of a fellow Jew, originally from Algeria, who ended up in Gabès as director of a bank. That was thirty years ago. I wish I had made a note of his name, which I can no longer remember.

In short, he became the president of the Community and took over its daily operations, and did such a good job of managing its meager resources that he worked a veritable miracle. At the end of his tenure, there was actually a surplus of exactly 727 francs. Everyone here can cite that figure. He refused to do restoration work on the synagogue or the bath, as he should have done, and instead, he did something truly extravagant. He bought himself a piece of land on the coast, one hundred thousand square meters of desert with his 727-franc fortune. It goes without saying that everything was done aboveboard and according to the rules.

When his job required that he move on to other shores, he bequeathed the title deed to his successor at a solemn ceremony at the synagogue, and had this to say: forty years from now, your children, or perhaps even yourselves, will cite my name in your prayers each and every day.

And indeed, a few years back, the military authorities purchased half this piece of land—I repeat, only half—for the tidy sum of six hundred thousand francs.

To what use did they put this treasure fallen from heaven? Opinion was so divided that they spent three years arguing over what to do. In the meantime, the bank account remained open and many, many hands found their way into it. At the end, only four hundred and five thousand francs remained. They realized that they were heading toward catastrophe, and decided they would buy up apartment buildings and rent them out, creating a source of income.

Thick as thieves, the committee members themselves sold the Community their useless, rundown properties that they were more than happy to be rid of, fetching high prices. And it is this very committee, composed of bearded elders and monkish schemers, that has been in power for twenty years and has never agreed to show the accounts to anyone.

Badly in need of repair, the Community's buildings were gradually abandoned by their tenants and now sit empty, a bad investment from the beginning that in the end yielded no returns.

.   .   .

It is a hot day for late September. Sudden showers cooled things off a bit yesterday, but a heat wave brought back high temperatures and humidity.

Swarms of flies accost you wherever you go. They cluster on everything, from the bread you've just sliced to the fruit you're about to put in your mouth. People say that this is their season: they appear with the ripening of the dates.

The dates of Gabès are not the best: smallish, pale, hard, and harsh on the tongue and palate. And yet, people here eat them. If they were left to ripen, they would rot. Jews and Bedouins seem to think they're delicious. They buy them by the donkey load, paying not per pound but by bunch, the number of which they can estimate at a glance.

At the market, piles of this fruit are spread out on the ground, next to quarters of meat that the Bedouins lay out on palm fronds, while the Jewish butchers, also outdoors, put theirs on chopping blocks. The sickening, fetid smell of raw flesh and sunbaked blood fills the air. Gathered around the butcher, who is sweating profusely, wiping his brow with the back of his hand, customers press against one another as they wait their turn. With a cutlass and hatchet, he manages to cut up the meat, or rather tear it apart, with some difficulty.

Shielded by a canopy fashioned out of jute sacks, many times patched and repatched, the Jewish merchants wait patiently for customers. What kind of wares are they selling? Whatever is required by the city-dwelling Arab and his country cousin farmer, the *fellah* from the *bled.** Everything from brightly colored cotton fabric to cheap combs, costume jewelry from Gablonz, and enameled pots and pans, not to mention candies, licorice sticks, and the thatch cord used to fetter livestock.

Their business is not an easy one, depending as it does on the whims of nature. It does actually rain here, once every five years, and if it comes at the wrong time, the date crop is ruined. Too bad; the Jew won't get paid his due this year either.

The Jew, the eternal scapegoat, has to work hard to scrape together a living. All week long, he goads his donkey over rocky roads from village to village with its load of cheap trinkets. He comes back to town on market day, having exchanged his goods for poultry, eggs, a goat, or a jar of oil.

He opens his little shop and waits. God often forgets him. But did the rabbi not say that we are in *galut,* exile? And that the Messiah will come—if not for us, then at least for our children? It must be true since the rabbi said so.

---

* That is, the peasant from the countryside.

Ask Yisaq, Braham, or Chemuel. They all have the same, resigned tone of those vanquished by life, or happy folk grown hopeless.

Now we come to the Jewish blacksmiths, a trade where Jews have the monopoly. All they know how to do is repair plowshares and other rudimentary farm tools. The Arabs, on the other hand, can produce fancy wrought-iron grillwork.

"Hello," I say to one of them. "May God come to your aid. How are you doing today?"

The hammering stops, the bellows cease their steady breathing, and a face looks up, completely black but for the white splash of teeth. He smiles and replies:

"Oh, hello there. You're the schoolteacher, aren't you? You're performing a true mitzvah [good deed] here, a true mitzvah. I'll be sending my three boys, after the holidays, God willing."

This is the way it was with everyone I met. They all had hopes that their children would be educated at their own school, sheltered from persecution.

. . .

That morning, we had an appointment at eleven with the president of the Community at the chief rabbi's yeshiva. But at ten, there was already a huge crowd massing in the cul-de-sac where the Talmud Torah school is located. Among them were parents of the children who would attend the school, but also Jews from the European quarter whose children were attending high school in Sousse or Tunis.

People were placing bets as to whether or not the rabbi would show. Same for the committee members, who were nowhere in sight. No, wait, here comes the president, along with two of his colleagues. Does he have rheumatism, or is he limping? Because he's walking with crutches, with some difficulty.

Just then, it's announced that the chief rabbi is busy with some guests and won't be coming. Fine, they say. They can carry on without him.

We pile into the classrooms of the Talmud Torah school. Fortunately, the rooms open onto one another, so that everyone in side rooms can hear the proceedings taking place in the middle room, if they stand on tiptoe or sit on someone's shoulders.

The president opens the session and declares what everyone knows already, which is that the Alliance is prepared to open a school for the Jews of Gabès, under conditions they never thought possible. All the Alliance asks, in fact, is for the local Community to provide a suitable building and ensure the teaching of Hebrew.

"But as you know, my friends," continued the president, "we are a poor Community, and we neither can provide a building nor afford to rent one. And as for the rabbis, if they are expected to teach at the school, then who will slaughter the chickens, who will attend the prayers of the sick, of women giving birth, of people on their deathbed?"

Voices of protest rise from the crowd. Everyone wants to talk at once. I try to restore some order and assure them that they will all get a chance to have their say.

I'll gloss over the comments made by the simple folk, who all offered more-or-less-practical solutions, and will elaborate on a statement made by a fervent Zionist, local leader of the Revisionists (the Jabotinsky party).* He is a young man, a jeweler by trade, and has travelled even as far as Algeria, which is something of an exploit for the parochial Gabès locals. He says to the president:

"Mr. Danon here wrote you a letter some six months ago announcing his visit to Gabès. In it, he stated the conditions under which the Alliance was prepared to provide a school for the town. First of all, you kept this letter a secret, even though it had great interest for us all. And secondly, you didn't even have the common courtesy to respond to Mr. Danon's letter.

This strange behavior astonishes us. On the one hand, you say that the Alliance's conditions are better than we could have dreamt, and on the other, you say that the Community does not have the means to meet these conditions. It's time you told us what you really think. Do you or do

---

* On Jabotinksy and the Revisionist movement, see note 22 of the introduction.

you not want the Alliance to open a school here? Do you or do you not want our children to be educated? If you do, then, consider it done. But if you don't, let it be known that all of us gathered here will form our own, independent, committee and do everything we can to make it happen.

And now, Mr. President, would you ask everyone who knows how to sign his name in French to please raise his hand? You see, apart from me, no one. And since you're in the money business, tell us if there is a single Jewish employee in any of the five banks in Gabès. Not a one, they are all Arabs. Well, I am here to predict that, in ten years' time, if you fail to open this school, the Jews are going to be the servants of the Arabs. And you all remember what our parents told us about life during the era of the beys: for Jews, it is the lowliest human condition."

But the chief rabbi has just arrived. Everyone rises. Those fortunate enough to be in his path grope for his hand or grab the hem of his garment to kiss. He sits down cross-legged, pulls out a handkerchief from deep within one of his pockets, spreads it over his knees, inserts a pinch of snuff into his mouth, coughs, blows his nose, and finally, aloof and full of contempt, asks almost offhandedly what we've been up to, what we have decided.

No one replies. I break the silence, saying: "Rabbi, how can we make a decision in your absence? We were waiting, since we were sure you would be coming. Everyone here wants to know whether you would oppose the opening of this school. For nothing will be done without your prior approval. Tell us, what serious reasons could drive you to thwart the desire of your flock? Remember that these are your children. . . ."

He interrupts: "My children? If they had the slightest respect for me, they would pay me my fees. I'll have you know that for the past fifteen months, I have been living on my personal income."

Here, the president interrupts: "Rabbi, you are shaming us!"

"I don't care if I am. Fifteen months! And you dare come ask that I provide a building, that I pay for rabbis. . . ."

I venture the question: if the Alliance were to provide for everything, would you accept the opening of this school?

"I will yield, but on one condition: that the Torah be given precedence over secular education. The Torah first and foremost."

"Two hours of Hebrew per day?"

"Not enough."

"And what if we divided the day into two parts: three hours in Hebrew and three in French? I am speaking on my own authority; I'll have to write to the Alliance."

Everyone cries out: "Rabbi, don't be so harsh. Say *tizku l'mitzvot*, say it!"*

The chief rabbi rises, order is quickly restored, and he deigns to reply: "Once Sukkot is over, I will write you a letter in which I will ask that you pay me what I'm owed. I will give you a month. If by that time you do not pay up, then I'll pack my things and head home. And it will be tough luck for you. Do you hear me, young and old? It will be tough luck for you.

Well, that's settled, then. As for the school, I cannot give my approval, but I will not stand in your way, as long as you respect my one condition, that the Torah always come first. I'll be on my way now. May peace be upon you."

And the crowd parts to let him pass.

.   .   .

It is nearly one o'clock when the meeting at the yeshiva comes to an end. Discussions continue in the street. People surround me: don't leave yet, Sir, they say. All is not lost. You saw that the rabbi is not opposed to the creation of the school. We'll set up a committee that is separate from the Charity Committee. Stay one more day, and help us get ourselves organized.

We decide to meet that same evening, at the law office of a fellow Jew in the European quarter, attorney Émile S., the only person capable of getting the job done.

---

* Literally, "Pay it forward!" The expression is uttered after someone does a mitzvah, a commandment or good deed, and implies that the actor should merit more mitzvot in the future.

A young but wise man, Émile S. experiences his Jewishness very keenly, even though he is completely disengaged from religion. He runs a major local business. As the son of a former president of the Community, he is well acquainted with internal Jewish matters.

His brother, who studied at your school in Tunis, is forever praising his teachers there, saying that they made him the man he is today.

Our meeting that evening starts at six and isn't over until nine. I am asked question after question about the Alliance, its origins, its founders, its schools in the Middle East and Morocco, its curricula, apprenticeships, its meal programs, its teachers' training school.

A whole new world is opening up for these people.

A committee is immediately formed to address the issue of rent: it will be paid for by student tuition. A quick calculation arrives at three hundred francs per month, just enough to cover it.

The same committee proposes a fund-raising campaign in town—which I am urged to attend in person—to pay for the school furnishings. Counting four classrooms of twenty benches each, at a cost of a hundred francs per bench, eight thousand will have to be raised by the little town of Gabès. And that does not include the inevitable remodeling work on the building itself.

The group's general enthusiasm makes light of the difficulties I'm pointing out.

But what about the rabbis, the teachers of the Torah? Who will pay them? This is the one sticking point.

If we assume that the Tunisian government will be granting a subsidy to the school of around thirty thousand francs, then twenty-four thousand should be enough to pay a couple of adjuncts, with the rest going to remunerate one of the rabbis. And the schoolchildren's parents will put pressure on the Charity Committee to come up with the other Hebrew teacher's salary.

School supplies, as is the case in all secular schools, will be paid for by the pupils themselves.

Conclusion

Below are a few personal reflections, by way of conclusion.

Your school in Gabès is as good as established at this point. Its operation will depend largely on the central committee.

1) Before all else, are you in a position to obtain approval to open this school?

I think you are liable to come up against a lot of ill will and incomprehension. The Secular Teachers' Union, which has a say in the matter, will most certainly oppose it, not to mention other adversaries waiting in the wings. They will object that there are already three classrooms set aside for Jewish pupils and that your school will interfere with the state school that has just been built at great cost.

You will have to explain that the state school, located way out of town, is practically inaccessible to Jewish children; that when they attempt to make the trek, they have to cross through vacant lots and cemeteries, where Arab children pelt them with stones; and that the security authorities, weary of policing this situation, just look the other way while the Jewish children suffer all sorts of harassment.

2) Every year, we fight to get the Tunisian government to raise its subsidy for the staff of your schools in Tunis, Sousse, and Sfax, which are currently underfunded. We earn much less than our colleagues in the state schools, whose concerns and responsibilities are far fewer than ours. It is always at the last minute that the board or the Resident General manages to come up with a few thousand francs to be spread over seventy or eighty instructors.

This year in particular, with steep rises in the cost of living, we will be asking for a sizable amount from the Resident General.

Will we have the courage to ask for another thirty thousand francs for the school in Gabès, in addition to all our other demands?

This is a matter of conscience for us all. Will we only look after our own personal interests, and leave our brothers in Gabès to fend for themselves as best they can, or will we overcome our selfishness and turn to them to extend a helping hand and take them under the welcoming wing of the Alliance?

I know how I would answer that question, but I speak only for myself, and cannot represent all my colleagues at the Alliance of Tunisia. I do not have the right to act in their name; I do not know them.

Devotedly,

V. Danon

A SWAN SONG, 1963

In this letter, written to the president of the Alliance Israélite Universelle in 1963, Danon reviews his career and reflects on his achievements, and those of the organization, in Tunisia. Tunisia had been an independent nation for seven years at the time of Danon's writing; he was seventy-two years old and but six years from his death. Perhaps it was with an eye to his own mortality that Danon wrote this letter, representing himself as "one of the last remaining witnesses to the miraculous accomplishments" of the AIU. Strikingly, the letter does not simply laud the AIU's successes (as well as Danon's own), but also bemoans the many challenges AIU employees experienced, including chronic underfunding. Among the achievements that Danon draws attention to is his writing, including a two-volume history of the Jews of Tunisia and sociological studies of the hara, or Jewish district. In his work as an author, and insofar as he remained in North Africa after Tunisian independence (having married a Tunisian Jewish woman and raised children in Sfax), Danon was unique among AIU employees.

Vitalis Danon
1 Rue Capitaine Madon
Tunis

Tunis, 4 February 1963
To the president of the Alliance Israélite Universelle
Paris

Mr. President,

I am honored to hereby acknowledge receipt of your letter dated 3 January, postmarked Nice.

I apologize for my delay in responding to the congratulations you so kindly extended on behalf of the Alliance Israélite to mark my promotion to the National Order of the Legion of Honor.[*] But my poor state of health has precluded an earlier response.

Indeed, for the past three years, my legs have been paralyzed, as has

---

[*] Established in 1802 under Emperor Napoleon Bonaparte, the National Order of the Legion of Honor (*Ordre National de la Légion d'Honneur*) is the highest distinction awarded in France for military or civil service to the nation.

my right arm, despite the unremitting efforts of my doctors. I am barely able to sign my name.

I am one of the last remaining witnesses to the miraculous accomplishments of the Alliance Israélite's educational mission among the Jewish communities of ancient Turkey in Europe and in the Middle East.* I say miraculous, for with very little funding, only small weekly contributions and occasional fund-raising drives, our school program managed to lift thousands upon thousands of Jews out of abject ignorance, saving them from what would have been a life of utter mediocrity had it not been for the Alliance's work.

The Alliance Israélite succeeded in designing and implementing what normally would require the concerted backing of an organized and fully funded state government.

The Alliance Israélite has been fortunate to include among its teachers an elite corps that wholeheartedly embraced and embodied all the values to which the mission is dedicated.

Hard-liners from a variety of constituencies were opposed to our schools at first, claiming that the lay education we provided alongside our religious instruction would somehow secularize the children placed in our charge.

Speaking for myself, I came to understand the Bible only when our Hebrew teacher finally dropped all the Judeo-Spanish jargon and adopted the infinitely more intelligible French translation by Zadok Kahn, the Grand Rabbi of France.

The Alliance Israélite thrived because it trusted the leadership of its directors.

I have always pointed to the example of Y. D. Semach, who had schools built in Morocco; Cazès; Navon; Confino; Tajouri; and many others that I will not enumerate for fear of leaving one out.† In all modesty, I can say I have followed in the path forged by my forerunners.

---

* "Ancient Turkey in Europe" refers to Ottoman Anatolia and the Balkans, sometimes called the "European provinces of the Ottoman Empire."

† Danon points, here, to other servants of the AIU, some of whom created schools for the organi-

Allow me to give a brief account of what I accomplished during my time at the head of your Tunisian schools.

I introduced the study of Arabic long before independence.

I initiated far-reaching reforms in the teaching of Hebrew. Until then, lessons in Jewish history had been left to the individual instructor's discretion, which resulted in a hodgepodge of legends and half-truths.

So, I rolled up my sleeves and wrote two small volumes of Jewish history, according to the most up-to-date methodology.

The books were a resounding success.

My research on the Tunis *hara* appeared in *Les Cahiers de Tunisie, Revue des sciences humaines*, published by the *Institut des Hautes Études de Tunis*. If I'm not mistaken, this sociological document caught the attention of UNESCO.

And here I am now, at the end of my career, worn to the bone, nerves utterly frayed.

It isn't easy, heading up such a sizable group of schools with so many pressing needs. The task required total devotion and asked that we give it our all.

Mr. President, you have acknowledged the value of my lifetime of work by obtaining for me the prestigious Legion of Honor. Please accept, Mr. President, my most heartfelt gratitude.

Vitalis Danon

---

zation. Notably, a number of these individuals were also lay scholars of North African and Middle Eastern Jewries, including Yomtov David Semach, who published a book in 1931 about his travels through the Jewish communities of the Middle East; David Cazès, who, in the late nineteenth century, wrote historical essays on Tunisian Jewry; and Albert Confino, who created vignettes about Algerian Jewry in the nineteen-forties.

ACKNOWLEDGMENTS

Bringing *Ninette of Sin Street* to an English-speaking audience has been nothing if not a group effort and a labor of love. The talents and generosity of Jane Kuntz, *Ninette*'s translator and interpreter, have been fundamental to this project; indeed, they are its bedrock.

The Alliance Israélite Universelle in Paris has been a partner in this endeavor, and we would like to recognize Jean-Claude Kuperminc, director of the AIU library, as well as Rose Levyne and Raoul Bellaïche, for their responsiveness and support. Many of the photographs and all of Danon's letters appear here with the permission of the AIU.

Guy Dugas, whose expertise in Tunisian-French literature is unparalleled, has been a valuable interlocutor. We would also like to thank Josh Lambert, Aron Rodrigue, Patrick Coleman, and Olivia Harrison, all of whom read versions of the introduction and provided expert feedback. This project benefited further from the keen reviews of anonymous reviewers. The manuscript has been immeasurably improved thanks to their questions and comments.

Chris Silver provided invaluable expertise on the nineteen-thirties music scene in colonial Tunisia. Bill Nelson ably produced the maps included in this volume, and Julia Phillips Cohen generously agreed to allow us to repurpose a map from *Sephardi Lives: A Documentary History, 1700–1950* (Stanford University Press, 2014), a book she co-edited with Sarah Stein. Greg Cohen helped ready our images for publication with skill and generosity. We are thankful to Dinah Diwan, an artist of tremendous imagination and zeal, for the evocative rendering of Ninette that graces this book's cover.

Afifa and Samir Marzouki were our gracious hosts and guides during a 2009 research stint in Tunis. Our conversations had an important impact on our vision of Judeo-Tunisian history and culture. Joshua Schreier, fellow traveler, also deserves our thanks for his company and insights.

The translation of *Ninette* was generously supported by a Ross Collaborative Grant through the Center for Jewish Studies at UCLA. Research support was provided through the UCLA Faculty Senate's Faculty Grants Program and by the Maurice Amado Chair in Sephardic Studies.

The entire staff at Stanford University Press has been a delight to work with. We are grateful to Micah O'Brien Siegel, Marie Deer, and Anne Fuzellier Jain for their professionalism and expertise.

Finally, we would like to offer our appreciation to Kate Wahl at Stanford University Press for her energetic support of *Ninette* and her editorial acumen.

Lia Brozgal and Sarah Abrevaya Stein

NOTES

1. *Ninette of Sin Street* belongs to an inaugural wave of Tunisian literature in French. A subset of Francophone literature (a category used to describe works by authors hailing from areas formerly colonized by France), the Tunisian-French literary tradition includes Jews (among them Chochana Boukobza, Claude Kayat, Albert Memmi, Georges Memmi, Nine Moatti, Serge Moatti, and Gilbert Naccache); Muslims (including Tahar Bekri, Abdelwahab Meddeb, and Mustapha Tlili); and authors of Sicilian and Maltese descent (such as Cesare Luccio and Mario Scalési).

2. H. Z. Hirschberg, *History of the Jews in North Africa*, vol. 2, *From the Ottoman Conquests to the Present Time* (Leiden: Brill, 1981), 82–83, 97–100, 137–139; Lionel Lévy, *La nation juive portugaise: Livourne, Amsterdam, Tunis, 1591–1951* (Paris: Harmattan, 1999); Minna Rozen, "The Livornese Jewish Merchants in Tunis and the Commerce with Marseilles at the End of the Seventeenth Century," *Michael* 9 (1985): 87–129; Haim Saadoun, "Tunisia," in *The Jews of the Middle East and North Africa in Modern Times*, ed. Reeva Spector Simon, Michael Menachem Laskier, and Sara Reguer (New York: Columbia University Press, 2003), 444–457; Paul Sebag, *Histoire des Juifs de Tunisie: des origines à nos jours* (Paris: L'Harmattan, 1991); Jacques Taieb, "Les Juifs Livournais de 1600 à 1881," in *Histoire communautaire, histoire plurielle: La communauté juive de Tunisie* (Tunis: Centre de Publications Universitaire, 1999), 153–164; Keith Walters, "Education for Jewish Girls in Late Nineteenth- and Early Twentieth-Century Tunis and the Spread of French in Tunisia," in *Jewish Culture and Society in North Africa*, ed. Emily Gottreich and Daniel Schroeter (Bloomington: Indiana University Press, 2011), 257–281.

3. Julia Clancy-Smith, *Mediterraneans: North Africa and Europe in an Age of Migration* (Berkeley: University of California Press, 2011) and *Rebel and Saint: Muslim Notables, Populist Protest, Colonial Encounters (Algeria*

and Tunisia, 1800–1904) (Berkeley: University of California Press, 1994); Mary Dewhurst Lewis, *Divided Rule: Sovereignty and Empire in French Tunisia* (Berkeley: University of California Press, 2014).

4. Lewis, *Divided Rule*, 8. When the first French census was conducted in Tunisia, in 1921, the population was estimated at roughly two million inhabitants, the vast majority of them (1.8 million) Muslim. Counted in the 1921 census were also 85,000 Italians, 54,000 French, and 48,500 Jews. Robert Attal and Claude Sitbon, *Regards sur les Juifs de Tunisie* (Paris: Albin Michel, 1979), 289–292; Haim Saadoun, "Tunisia," *Encyclopedia of Jews in the Islamic World*, ed. Norman A. Stillman, Brill Online, 2016, accessed 3 June 2016, http://referenceworks.brillonline.com/entries/encyclopedia-of-jews-in-the-islamic-world/tunisia-COM_0021690.

5. Aron Rodrigue, *French Jews, Turkish Jews: The Alliance Israélite Universelle and the Politics of Jewish Schooling in Turkey 1860–1925* (Bloomington: Indiana University Press, 1992) and *Jews and Muslims: Images of Sephardi and Eastern Jewries in Modern Times* (Seattle: University of Washington Press, 2003); Walters, "Education."

6. Archives of the Alliance Israélite Universelle, Paris [hereafter, AIU] AH Tunisie E 111, letter by Vitalis Danon to the president of the AIU, 2 March 1921.

7. Rodrigue, *French Jews, Turkish Jews.*

8. Frances Malino, "'Adieu à ma maison': Sephardi Adolescent Identities, 1932–36," *Jewish Social Studies* 15/1 (Fall 2008): 131–145.

9. Haim Saadoun, "Sfax," in Stillman, *Encyclopedia of Jews in the Islamic World*, accessed 3 June 2016, http://referenceworks.brillonline.com/entries/encyclopedia-of-jews-in-the-islamic-world/sfax -COM_0019730; Joy Land, "Corresponding Women: Female Educators of the Alliance Israélite Universelle in Tunisia, 1882–1914," in Gottreich and Schroeter, *Jewish Culture and Society*, 239–257, here 243; Paul Sebag, *Histoire des Juifs de Tunisie: des origines à nos jours* (Paris: L'Harmattan, 1991).

10. AIU AH Tunisie E 50, letter by Vitalis Danon to the president of the AIU, 27 June 1918.

11. A translation of Danon's letter on this theme may be found in Rodrigue, *Jews and Muslims*, 226.

12. AIU AH Tunisie E III, letter by Vitalis Danon to the president of the AIU, 21 June 1920; 28 August 1920.

13. AIU AH Tunisie E III, letter by Vitalis Danon to the president of the AIU, 2 March, 1921.

14. AIU AM Tunisie E 31.

15. See "Vitalis Danon: éducateur et écrivain," in *Les Cahiers de l'Alliance Israélite Universelle* II (1995), 2. Several members of the Jewish community of Tunisia published firsthand accounts of life under Vichy and the German occupation; see Paul Ghez, *Six mois sous la botte* (Paris: Éditions Le Manuscrit, 2009; first pub. Tunis, 1943) and Robert Borgel, *Étoile jaune et croix gammée* (Paris: Éditions Le Manuscrit, 2007; first pub. Tunis, 1944). Claude Nataff's *Les Juifs de Tunisie sous le joug nazi* (Paris: Éditions Le Manuscrit, "Collection Témoignages de la Shoah," 2012) is a collection of primary sources and testimonials. For a scholarly treatment of Tunisia, Vichy, and the German occupation, see Jean-Pierre Allali, *Les Juifs de Tunisie sous la botte allemande* (Paris: Éditions Glyphe, 2014); Michel Abitbol, *The Jews of North Africa During the Second World War*, trans. Catherine Tihanyi Zentelis (Detroit: Wayne State University Press, 1989); and Michael Laskier, *North African Jewry in the Twentieth Century: The Jews of Morocco, Tunisia and Algeria* (New York: New York University Press, 1994).

16. Danon did have family in Istanbul and Salonica, and perhaps some remaining in Edirne. The AIU has not preserved whatever personal correspondences he might have maintained.

17. AIU Tunisie I.C.1, Vitalis Danon to the president of the AIU, 18 February 1932, translated and published in Rodrigue, *Jews and Muslims*, 225–228.

18. AIU AH Tunisie E III, Vitalis Danon to the president of the AIU, 3 June 1927; 25 June 1929; 1 and 7 October 1931.

19. See, for example AIU AH Tunisie E 50, letter by Vitalis Danon to the Comité de Bienfaisance Israélite de Sfax, 6 November 1927.

20. See, for example AIU AH Tunisie E 050, Vitalis Danon to the president of the AIU, 5 December 1935.

21. AIU AH Tunisie E 111, Vitalis Danon to the president of the AIU, 20 March 1930.

22. The paper was created and directed by Félix Allouche; its editors-in-chief were Henri Maarek and Elie Louzon. Based first in Sfax and, as of 1930, in Tunis, *Le Réveil Juif* was influenced by Revisionist Zionism, a radical branch of Zionism created in 1925 by Vladimir Ze'ev Jabotinksy, which advocated for the creation of a Jewish state in British-Mandate-ruled Palestine and encouraged militancy on the part of its followers. Mohsen Hamli, "Le Réveil Juif (Sfax)," in Stillman, *Encyclopedia of Jews in the Islamic World*, accessed 3 June 2016, http://referenceworks. brillonline.com/entries/encyclopedia-of-jews-in-the-islamic-world/le -reveil-juif-sfax-SIM_0013560; Laskier, *North African Jewry*; Laskier, "The Evolution of Zionist Activity in the Jewish Communities of Morocco, Tunisia, and Algeria: 1897–1947," *Studies in Zionism* 4.2 (1993): 205–23; Saadoun, "Tunisia" (2003).

23. See, for example, AIU AH Tunisie E 111, Vitalis Danon to the president of the AIU, 14 November 1929.

24. *Cahiers du Bétar* was another Tunisian Zionist newspaper, named after the Revisionist Zionist youth movement Betar, founded in 1932. Laskier, *North African Jewry*, 38.

25. Danielle Omer, "Contre la disparation du monde francophone de l'Alliance universelle israélite: les efforts de Vitalis Danon à Tunis (1945–1958)," *Documents pour l'histoire du français langue étrangère ou seconde*, accessed 12 December 2015, http://www.dhfles.revues.org/121.

26. Lucette Valensi and Nathan Wachtel, *Jewish Memories* (Berkeley: University of California Press, 1991).

27. The notion of the "genius" of the French language dates to the sixteenth century; such ideas became even more powerful during the Enlightenment, particularly as articulated by writers like Rivarol, who famously declared "if it is not clear, it is not French." Antoine de Rivarol, "De l'universalité de la langue française," speech given in Berlin in 1784.

Available through Gallica, the catalog of the Bibliothèque nationale de France.

28. Walters, "Education," 274 and Table 17.4.

29. Rodrigue, *Jews and Muslims*, 26–27.

30. "The Challenge Posed by the New French Presence in Tunisia, 1881," letter in Rodrigue, *Jews and Muslims*, 179–181.

31. Jacques Véhel (pseudonym of Jacques-Victor Lévy) and Ryvel (pseudonym of Raphaël Lévy, Jacques's nephew) both belonged to the influential Lévy family, descended from Galician Jews who had arrived in Tunisia in the early nineteenth century. Ryvel's father, Zriki, directed the Imprimerie Finzi, one of the oldest presses in Tunisia (founded 1829). The press was known and well respected for its promotion of interfaith tolerance, manifested in its technical capacity to print in Arabic, Latin, Hebrew and Cyrillic characters, and through its promotion of a multicultural, multiethnic, polyglot work environment.

32. The novel was published serially in the Parisian magazine *L'Ère nouvelle* (August 1926).

33. See Guy Dugas, "L'école de Tunis et le développement de la littérature judeo-maghrébine dans l'entre-deux guerres," *Cahiers d'études maghrébines* 3 (1991): 80–86. For a more broadly contextualized study in English, see Dugas and Patricia Geesey, "An Unknown Maghrebian Genre: Judeo-Maghrebian Literature of French Expression," *Research in African Literatures* 23/2 (1992): 21–32.

34. Vitalis Danon, Jacques Véhel, and Ryvel, *La hara conte: folklore judéo-tunisien* (Paris: Éditions Ivrit, 1929); Jacques Véhel, Ryvel, Jules Lellouche, and V. Guérassimoff, *Le bestiaire du ghetto* (Tunis: Société des Écrivains de l'Afrique du Nord, 1934). In the greater North African context, the writers of the Tunis School were preceded only by the Algerian-Jewish novelist Sadia Lévy, who published *Rabbin* (Paris, 1886) and *XI journées en force* (Algiers, 1901), both co-written with French writer Robert Randeau. Within Tunisia, there exists a long tradition of Jewish literature in Judeo-Arabic. Published material consists primarily of translations of liturgy, although folktales (generally transmitted orally)

were occasionally introduced into religious publications. See Yosef Tobi and Tsivia Tovi, *Judeo-Arabic Literature in Tunisia, 1850–1950* (Detroit: Wayne State University Press, 2014), 16.

35. The multicultural "ghetto" is on display in *Ninette*, as well as in other contemporary Francophone Judeo-Tunisian literature. See Nine Moatti, *Belles de Tunis* (Paris: Seuil, 1983). For a fictional representation of the Algerian Jewish quarter, see Blanche Bendahan's award-winning novel *Mazaltob* (Paris: Éditions du Tambourin, 1930). On the history of the *hara* and mellah as lived spaces see, among other sources, Paul Sebag, *L'évolution d'un ghetto nord-africain: la hara de Tunis* (Paris: Presses Universitaires de France, 1959); Emily Benichou Gottreich, *The Mellah of Marrakesh: Jewish and Muslim Space in Morocco's Red City* (Bloomington: Indiana University Press, 2007); Susan Miller, "The Mellah of Fez: Reflections on the Spatial Turn in Moroccan Jewish History," in *Jewish Topographies: Visions of Space, Traditions of Place*, ed. A. Nocke, J. Brauch, and A. Lipphardt (London: Ashgate, 2008).

36. Danon, "Un enfant de la Hara," in *La hara conte*, 62–65.

37. Guy Dugas, "Vitalis Danon et l'art de la novella," Postface to *Ninette de la rue du Péché* (Paris: Collection Pages de l'Alliance/Éditions Le Manuscrit, 2007), 202. Dugas observes that Maghrebi Jews tended to have deep, established relationships with local journalists and the press, which provided a natural outlet for short-form literature. See Guy Dugas, *Bibliographie critique de la littérature judeo-maghrébine d'expression française (1896–1999)* (Paris: L'Harmattan, 1992), 11–12.

38. Dugas, Postface, 111–112.

39. Danon, Véhel, and Ryvel, *La hara conte*, 151. The word *goys*—derived from the Hebrew word for "nation" and long used to designate "non-Jews"—appears in the original as reproduced here, in italics, using an -s for the plural form rather than the Hebrew plural, *goyim*.

40. Abraham L. Udovitch and Lucette Valensi, *The Last Arab Jews: The Communities of Jerba, Tunisia* (New York: Harwood Academic, 1984).

41. Rodrigue, *Jews and Muslims*, 199.

42. In addition to *Le roman de la Manoubia*, mentioned above, he

published *Aron le colporteur: nouvelle juive nord-africaine* in 1933, under the imprint Éditions de la Kahena, in Tunis, and *Dieu a pardonné: nouvelle juive nord-africaine* under the same imprint in 1934. None of Danon's novels received critical attention during his lifetime; only *Ninette* was identified for reissue by the AIU.

43. In addition to Danon's "Un enfant du ghetto" in *La hara conte*, 59–65, see Ryvel, "Keppara," *La hara conte*, 91–98, and *L'enfant d'Oukala et autres contes de la hara* (Tunis: La Kahéna, 1931; 2nd ed. Paris: JC Lattès, 1980).

44. Rodrigue, *Jews and Muslims*, 72.

45. Beginning in the nineteenth century, across North Africa and internationally, Jewish prostitution was both a real phenomenon and a recurrent theme in the literature of many languages, including Yiddish.

46. This is an oft-repeated conceit of Jewish literature that has been explored by, among others, Dan Miron and Ruth Wisse, the latter of whom has spoken of the "compressed intimacy and the cultural intricacy" implicit in such renderings. Ruth Wisse, *I. L. Peretz and the Making of Modern Jewish Culture* (Seattle: University of Washington Press, 1991), 21.

47. Saadoun, "Tunisia" (2003).

48. Memmi has discussed the conditions of his departure in several book-length personal essays, including *Ce que je crois* (Paris: Grasset, 1985), *Le nomade immobile* (Paris: Arléa, 2000), and *Testament insolent* (Paris: Éditions Odile Jacob, 2010).

CONTRIBUTORS

Vitalis Danon (1897–1957), born in Edirne (Adrianople) in the Ottoman Empire, spent much of his life in Sfax, Tunisia. A novelist, teacher, and school director for the Alliance Israélite Universelle, he is best known for *Ninette of Sin Street*, his last work of fiction.

Lia Brozgal is Associate Professor of French and Francophone Studies at UCLA. She is the author of *Against Autobiography: Albert Memmi and the Production of Theory* (2013) and coeditor of *Being Contemporary: French Literature, Culture and Politics Today* (2016). She is currently completing a manuscript on literary and visual representations of the October 17, 1961 massacre of Algerian protestors in Paris. Her work has been recognized by the American Council of Learned Societies, the University of California Presidential Grants, and the Camargo Foundation.

Sarah Abrevaya Stein is Professor of History and Maurice Amado Chair in Sephardic Studies at UCLA. Her recent books include *Extraterritorial Dreams: European Citizenship, Sephardi Jews, and the Ottoman Twentieth Century* (2016), *Saharan Jews and the Fate of French Algeria* (2014), and *Sephardi Lives: A Documentary History, 1700–1950* (2014). With the support of a Guggenheim Fellowship, Stein is currently working on a book, to be published by Farrar, Straus, & Giroux, that offers an intimate history of a single Sephardi family along the arc of the twentieth century.

Jane Kuntz holds a doctorate in French from the University of Illinois and is a translator of French-language fiction and nonfiction. Recent translations include *A History of the Grandparents I Never Had*, by Ivan Jablonka (2016); *Islam and the Challenge of Civilization*, by Abdelwahab Meddeb (2013); and Meddeb's experimental first novel, *Talismano* (2011). Kuntz lived and worked in Tunisia from 1975 until 1993 as a teacher and translator and as an educational adviser for AMIDEAST-Tunis.